MALVINA OF BRITTANY

MALVINA OF BRITTANY

Jerome K. Jerome

Serenity
Publishers, LLC

ROCKVILLE, MARYLAND

2010

ISBN: 978-1-60450-765-2

Published by Serenity Publishers
An Arc Manor Company
P. O. Box 10339
Rockville, MD 20849-0339
www.SerenityPublishers.com

Printed in the United States of America/United Kingdom

CONTENTS

MALVINA OF BRITTANY

The Preface

T he Doctor never did believe this story, but claims for it that, to a great extent, it has altered his whole outlook on life.

"Of course, what actually happened—what took place under my own nose," continued the Doctor, "I do not dispute. And then there is the case of Mrs. Marigold. That was unfortunate, I admit, and still is, especially for Marigold. But, standing by itself, it proves nothing. These fluffy, giggling women—as often as not it is a mere shell that they shed with their first youth—one never knows what is underneath. With regard to the others, the whole thing rests upon a simple scientific basis. The idea was 'in the air,' as we say—a passing brain-wave. And when it had worked itself out there was an end of it. As for all this Jack-and-the-Beanstalk tomfoolery—"

There came from the darkening uplands the sound of a lost soul. It rose and fell and died away.

"Blowing stones," explained the Doctor, stopping to refill his pipe. "One finds them in these parts. Hollowed out during the glacial period. Always just about twilight that one hears it. Rush of air caused by sudden sinking of the temperature. That's how all these sort of ideas get started."

The Doctor, having lit his pipe, resumed his stride.

"I don't say," continued the Doctor, "that it would have happened without her coming. Undoubtedly it was she who supplied the necessary psychic conditions. There was that about her—a sort of atmosphere. That quaint archaic French of hers—King Arthur and the round table and Merlin; it seemed to recreate it all. An artful minx, that is the only explanation. But while she was looking at you, out of that curious aloofness of hers—"

The Doctor left the sentence uncompleted.

"As for old Littlecherry," the Doctor began again quite suddenly, "that's his speciality—folklore, occultism, all that flummery. If you knocked at his door with the original Sleeping Beauty on your arm he'd only fuss round her with cushions and hope that she'd had a good night. Found a seed once—chipped it out of an old fossil, and grew it in a pot in his study. About the most dilapidated weed you ever saw. Talked about it as if he had re-discovered the Elixir of Life. Even if he didn't say anything in actually so many words, there was the way he went about. That of itself was enough to have started the whole thing, to say nothing of that loony old Irish housekeeper of his, with her head stuffed full of elves and banshees and the Lord knows what."

Again the Doctor lapsed into silence. One by one the lights of the village peeped upward out of the depths. A long, low line of light, creeping like some luminous dragon across the horizon, showed the track of the Great Western express moving stealthily towards Swindon.

"It was altogether out of the common," continued the Doctor, "quite out of the common, the whole thing. But if you are going to accept old Littlecherry's explanation of it—"

The Doctor struck his foot against a long grey stone, half hidden in the grass, and only just saved himself from falling.

"Remains of some old cromlech," explained the Doctor. "Somewhere about here, if we were to dig down, we should find a withered bundle of bones crouching over the dust of a prehistoric luncheon-basket. Interesting neighbourhood!"

The descent was rough. The Doctor did not talk again until we had reached the outskirts of the village.

"I wonder what's become of them?" mused the Doctor. "A rum go, the whole thing. I should like to have got to the bottom of it."

We had reached the Doctor's gate. The Doctor pushed it open and passed in. He seemed to have forgotten me.

"A taking little minx," I heard him muttering to himself as he fumbled with the door. "And no doubt meant well. But as for that cock-and-bull story—"

I pieced it together from the utterly divergent versions furnished me by the Professor and the Doctor, assisted, so far as later incidents are concerned, by knowledge common to the village.

1—*The Story*

It commenced, so I calculate, about the year 2000 B.C., or, to be more precise—for figures are not the strong point of the old chroniclers—when King Heremon ruled over Ireland and Harbundia was Queen of the White Ladies of Brittany, the fairy Malvina being her favourite attendant. It is with Malvina that this story is chiefly concerned. Various quite pleasant happenings are recorded to her credit. The White Ladies belonged to the "good people," and, on the whole, lived up to their reputation. But in Malvina, side by side with much that is commendable, there appears to have existed a most reprehensible spirit of mischief, displaying itself in pranks that, excusable, or at all events understandable, in, say, a pixy or a pigwidgeon, strike one as altogether unworthy of a well-principled White Lady, posing as the friend and benefactress of mankind. For merely refusing to dance with her—at midnight, by the shores of a mountain lake; neither the time nor the place calculated to appeal to an elderly gentleman, suffering possibly from rheumatism—she on one occasion transformed an eminently respectable proprietor of tin mines into a nightingale, necessitating a change of habits that to a business man must have been singularly irritating. On another occasion a quite important queen, having had the misfortune to quarrel with Malvina over some absurd point of etiquette in connection with a lizard, seems, on waking the next morning, to have found herself changed into what one judges, from the somewhat vague description afforded by the ancient chroniclers, to have been a sort of vegetable marrow.

Such changes, according to the Professor, who is prepared to maintain that evidence of an historical nature exists sufficient to prove that the White Ladies formed at one time an actual living community, must be taken in an allegorical sense. Just as modern lunatics believe themselves to be china vases or poll-parrots, and think and behave as such, so it must have been easy, the Professor argues, for beings of superior intelligence to have exerted hypnotic influence upon the superstitious savages by whom they were surrounded, and who, intellectually considered, could have been little more than children.

"Take Nebuchadnezzar." I am still quoting the Professor. "Nowadays we should put him into a strait-waistcoat. Had he lived in Northern Europe instead of Southern Asia, legend would have told us how some Kobold or Stromkarl had turned him into a composite amalgamation of a serpent, a cat and a kangaroo." Be that as it may, this passion for change—in other people—seems to have grown upon Malvina until she must have become little short of a public nuisance, and eventually it landed her in trouble.

The incident is unique in the annals of the White Ladies, and the chroniclers dwell upon it with evident satisfaction. It came about through the betrothal of King Heremon's only son, Prince Gerbot, to the Princess Berchta of Normandy. Malvina seems to have said nothing, but to have bided her time. The White Ladies of Brittany, it must be remembered, were not fairies pure and simple. Under certain conditions they were capable of becoming women, and this fact, one takes it, must have exerted a disturbing influence upon their relationships with eligible male mortals. Prince Gerbot may not have been altogether blameless. Young men in those sadly unenlightened days may not, in their dealings with ladies, white or otherwise, have always been the soul of discretion and propriety. One would like to think the best of her.

But even the best is indefensible. On the day appointed for the wedding she seems to have surpassed herself. Into what particular shape or form she altered the wretched Prince Gerbot; or into what shape or form she persuaded him that he had been altered, it really, so far as the moral responsibility of Malvina is concerned, seems to be immaterial; the chronicle does not state: evidently something too indelicate for a self-respecting chronicler to even hint at. As, judging from other passages in the book, squeamishness does not seem to have been the author's literary failing, the sensitive reader can feel only grateful for the omission. It would have been altogether too harrowing.

It had, of course, from Malvina's point of view, the desired effect. The Princess Berchta appears to have given one look and then to have fallen fainting into the arms of her attendants. The marriage was postponed indefinitely, and Malvina, one sadly suspects, chortled. Her triumph was short-lived.

Unfortunately for her, King Heremon had always been a patron of the arts and science of his period. Among his friends were to be reckoned magicians, genii, the Nine Korrigans or Fays of Brittany—all sorts of parties capable of exerting influence, and, as events proved, only too willing. Ambassadors waited upon Queen Harbundia; and Harbundia, even had she wished, as on many previous occasions, to stand by her favourite, had no alternative. The fairy Malvina was called upon to return to Prince Gerbot his proper body and all therein contained.

She flatly refused. A self-willed, obstinate fairy, suffering from swelled head. And then there was that personal note. Merely that he should marry the Princess Berchta! She would see King Heremon, and Anniamus, in his silly old wizard's robe, and the Fays of Brittany, and all the rest of them—! A really nice White Lady may not have cared to finish the sentence, even to herself. One imagines the flash of the fairy eye, the stamp of the fairy foot. What could they do to her, any of them, with all their clacking of tongues and their wagging of heads? She, an immortal fairy! She would change Prince Gerbot back at a time of her own choosing. Let them attend to their own tricks and leave her to mind hers. One pictures long walks and talks between the distracted Harbundia and her refractory favourite—appeals to reason, to sentiment: "For my sake." "Don't you see?" "After all, dear, and even if he did."

It seems to have ended by Harbundia losing all patience. One thing there was she could do that Malvina seems either not to have known of or not to have anticipated. A solemn meeting of the White Ladies was convened for the night of the midsummer moon. The place of meeting is described by the ancient chroniclers with more than their usual exactitude. It was on the land that the magician Kalyb had, ages ago, raised up above all Brittany to form the grave of King Taramis. The "Sea of the Seven Islands" lay to the north. One guesses it to be the ridge formed by the Arree Mountains. "The Lady of the Fountain" appears to have been present, suggesting the deep green pool from which the river D'Argent takes its source. Roughly speaking, one would place it halfway between the modern towns of Morlaix and Callac. Pedestrians, even of the present day, speak of the still loneliness of that high plateau, treeless, houseless, with no sign of human hand there but that high, towering monolith round which the shrill winds moan incessantly. There, possibly on some broken fragment of those great grey stones, Queen Harbundia sat in judgment. And the judgment was—and from it there was no appeal—that the fairy Malvina should be cast out from among the community of the White Ladies of Brittany. Over the face of the earth she should wander, alone and unforgiven. Solemnly from the book of the roll-call of the White Ladies the name of Malvina was struck out for ever.

The blow must have fallen upon Malvina as heavily as it was unexpected. Without a word, without one backward look, she seems to have departed. One pictures the white, frozen face, the wide-open, unseeing eyes, the trembling, uncertain steps, the groping hands, the deathlike silence clinging like grave-clothes round about her.

From that night the fairy Malvina disappears from the book of the chroniclers of the White Ladies of Brittany, from legend and from folklore whatsoever. She does not appear again in history till the year A.D. 1914.

2——How It Came About

It was on an evening towards the end of June, 1914, that Flight Commander Raffleton, temporarily attached to the French Squadron then harboured at Brest, received instructions by wireless to return at once to the British Air Service Headquarters at Farnborough, in Hampshire. The night, thanks to a glorious full moon, would afford all the light he required, and young Raffleton determined to set out at once. He appears to have left the flying ground just outside the arsenal at Brest about nine o'clock. A little beyond Huelgoat he began to experience trouble with the carburettor. His idea at first was to push on to Lannion, where he would be able to secure expert assistance; but matters only getting worse, and noticing beneath him a convenient stretch of level ground, he decided to descend and attend to it himself. He alighted without difficulty and proceeded to investigate. The job took him, unaided, longer than he had anticipated. It was a warm, close night, with hardly a breath of wind, and when he had finished he was feeling hot and tired. He had drawn on his helmet and was on the point of stepping into his seat, when the beauty of the night suggested to him that it would be pleasant, before starting off again, to stretch his legs and cool himself a little. He lit a cigar and looked round about him.

The plateau on which he had alighted was a table-land standing high above the surrounding country. It stretched around him, treeless, houseless. There was nothing to break the lines of the horizon but a group of gaunt grey stones, the remains, so he told himself, of some ancient menhir, common enough to the lonely desert lands of Brittany. In general the stones lie overthrown and scattered, but this particular specimen had by some strange chance remained undisturbed through all the centuries. Mildly interested, Flight Commander Raffleton strolled leisurely towards it. The moon was at its zenith. How still the quiet night must have been was impressed upon him by the fact that he distinctly heard, and counted, the strokes of a church clock which must have been at least six miles away. He remembers looking at his watch and noting that there was a slight difference between his own and the church time. He made it eight minutes past twelve. With the dying away of the last vibrations of the distant bell the silence and the solitude of the place seemed to return and settle down upon it with increased insistence. While he was working it had not troubled him, but beside the black shadows thrown by those hoary stones it had the effect almost of a presence. It was with a sense of relief that he contemplated returning to his machine and starting up his engine. It would whir and buzz and give back to him a comfortable feeling of life and security. He would walk round the stones just once and then be off. It was wonderful how they had defied old Time. As they had been placed there, quite possibly ten thousand years ago, so they still stood, the altar of that vast, empty sky-roofed temple. And while he was gazing at them, his cigar between his lips, struggling with a strange forgotten impulse that was tugging at his knees, there came from the very heart of the great grey stones the measured rise and fall of a soft, even breathing.

Young Raffleton frankly confesses that his first impulse was to cut and run. Only his soldier's training kept his feet firm on the heather. Of course, the explanation was simple. Some animal had made the place its nest. But then what animal was ever known to sleep so soundly as not to be disturbed by human footsteps? If wounded, and so unable to escape, it would not be breathing with that quiet, soft regularity, contrasting so strangely with the stillness and the silence all round. Possibly an owl's nest. Young owlets make that sort of noise—the "snorers," so country people call them. Young Raffleton threw away his cigar and went down upon his knees to grope among the shadows, and, doing so, he touched something warm and soft and yielding.

But it wasn't an owl. He must have touched her very lightly, for even then she did not wake. She lay there with her head upon her arm. And now close to her, his eyes growing used to the shadows, he saw her quite plainly, the wonder of the parted lips, the gleam of the white limbs beneath their flimsy covering.

Of course, what he ought to have done was to have risen gently and moved away. Then he could have coughed. And if that did not wake her he might have touched her lightly, say, on the shoulder, and have called to her, first softly, then a little louder, "Mademoiselle," or "Mon enfant." Even better, he might have stolen away on tiptoe and left her there sleeping.

This idea does not seem to have occurred to him. One makes the excuse for him that he was but three-and-twenty, that, framed in the purple moonlight, she seemed to him the most beautiful creature his eyes had ever seen. And then there was the brooding mystery of it all, that atmosphere of far-off primeval times from which the roots of life still draw their sap. One takes it he forgot that he was Flight Commander Raffleton, officer and gentleman; forgot the proper etiquette applying to the case of ladies found sleeping upon lonely moors without a chaperon. Greater still, the possibility that he never thought of anything at all, but, just impelled by a power beyond himself, bent down and kissed her.

Not a platonic kiss upon the brow, not a brotherly kiss upon the cheek, but a kiss full upon the parted lips, a kiss of worship and amazement, such as that with which Adam in all probability awakened Eve.

Her eyes opened, and, just a little sleepily, she looked at him. There could have been no doubt in her mind as to what had happened. His lips were still pressing hers. But she did not seem in the least surprised, and most certainly not angry. Raising herself to a sitting posture, she smiled and held out her hand that he might help her up. And, alone in that vast temple, star-roofed and moon-illumined, beside that grim grey altar of forgotten rites, hand in hand they stood and looked at one another.

"I beg your pardon," said Commander Raffleton. "I'm afraid I have disturbed you."

He remembered afterwards that in his confusion he had spoken to her in English. But she answered him in French, a quaint, old-fashioned French such as one rarely finds but in the pages of old missals. He would have had some difficulty in translating it literally, but the meaning of it was, adapted to our modern idiom:

"Don't mention it. I'm so glad you've come."

He gathered she had been expecting him. He was not quite sure whether he ought not to apologise for being apparently a little late. True, he had no recollection of any such appointment. But then at that particular moment Commander Raffleton may be said to have had no consciousness of anything beyond just himself and the wondrous other beside him. Somewhere outside was moonlight and a world; but all that seemed unimportant. It was she who broke the silence.

"How did you get here?" she asked.

He did not mean to be enigmatical. He was chiefly concerned with still gazing at her.

"I flew here," he answered. Her eyes opened wider at that, but with interest, not doubt.

"Where are your wings?" she asked. She was leaning sideways, trying to get a view of his back.

He laughed. It made her seem more human, that curiosity about his back.

"Over there," he answered. She looked, and for the first time saw the great shimmering sails gleaming like silver under the moonlight.

She moved towards it, and he followed, noticing without surprise that the heather seemed to make no sign of yielding to the pressure of her white feet.

She halted a little away from it, and he came and stood beside her. Even to Commander Raffleton himself it looked as if the great wings were quivering, like the outstretched pinions of a bird preening itself before flight.

"Is it alive?" she asked.

"Not till I whisper to it," he answered. He was losing a little of his fear of her. She turned to him.

"Shall we go?" she asked.

He stared at her. She was quite serious, that was evident. She was to put her hand in his and go away with him. It was all settled. That is why he had come. To her it did not matter where. That was his affair. But where he went she was to go. That was quite clearly the programme in her mind.

To his credit, let it be recorded, he did make an effort. Against all the forces of nature, against his twenty-three years and the red blood pulsing in his veins, against the fumes of the midsummer moonlight encompassing him and the voices of the stars, against the demons of poetry and romance and mystery chanting their witches' music in his ears, against the marvel and the glory of her as she stood beside him, clothed in the purple of the night, Flight Commander Raffleton fought the good fight for common sense.

Young persons who, scantily clad, go to sleep on the heather, five miles from the nearest human habitation, are to be avoided by well-brought-up young officers of His Majesty's Aerial Service. The incidence of their being uncannily beautiful and alluring should serve as an additional note of warning. The girl had had a row with her mother and wanted to get away. It was this infernal moonlight that was chiefly responsible. No wonder dogs bayed at it. He almost fancied he could hear one now. Nice, respectable, wholesome-minded things, dogs. No damned sentiment about them. What if he had kissed her! One is not bound for life to every woman one kisses. Not the first time she had been kissed, unless all the young men in Brittany were blind or white blooded. All this pretended innocence and simplicity! It was just put on. If not, she must be a lunatic. The proper thing to do was to say good-bye with a laugh and a jest, start up his machine and be off to England—dear old practical, merry England, where he could get breakfast and a bath.

It wasn't a fair fight; one feels it. Poor little prim Common Sense, with her defiant, turned-up nose and her shrill giggle and her innate vulgarity. And against her the stillness of the night, and the music of the ages, and the beating of his heart.

So it all fell down about his feet, a little crumbled dust that a passing breath of wind seemed to scatter, leaving him helpless, spellbound by the magic of her eyes.

"Who are you?" he asked her.

"Malvina," she answered him. "I am a fairy."

3——How Cousin Christopher Became Mixed Up With It

It did just occur to him that maybe he had not made that descent quite as successfully as he had thought he had; that maybe he had come down on his head; that in consequence he had done with the experiences of Flight Commander Raffleton and was now about to enter on a new and less circumscribed existence. If so, the beginning, to an adventuresome young spirit, seemed promising. It was Malvina's voice that recalled him from this train of musing.

"Shall we go?" she repeated, and this time the note in her voice suggested command rather than question.

Why not? Whatever had happened to him, at whatever plane of existence he was now arrived, the machine apparently had followed him. Mechanically he started it up. The familiar whir of the engine brought back to him the possibility of his being alive in the ordinary acceptation of the term. It also suggested to him the practical advisability of insisting that Malvina should put on his spare coat. Malvina being five feet three, and the coat having been built for a man of six feet one, the effect under ordinary circumstances would have been comic. What finally convinced Commander Raffleton that Malvina really was a fairy was that, in that coat, with the collar standing up some six inches above her head, she looked more like one than ever.

Neither of them spoke. Somehow it did not seem to be needed. He helped her to climb into her seat and tucked the coat about her feet. She answered by the same smile with which she had first stretched out her hand to him. It was just a smile of endless content, as if all her troubles were now over. Commander Raffleton sincerely hoped they were. A momentary flash of intelligence suggested to him that his were just beginning.

Commander Raffleton's subconscious self it must have been that took charge of the machine. He seems, keeping a few miles inland, to have followed the line of the coast to a little south of the Hague lighthouse. Thereabouts he remembers descending for the purpose of replenishing his tank. Not having anticipated a passenger, he had filled up before starting with a spare supply of petrol, an incident that was fortunate. Malvina appears to have been interested in watching what she probably regarded as some novel breed of dragon being nourished from tins extricated from under her feet, but to have accepted this, together with all other details of the flight, as in the natural scheme of things. The monster refreshed, tugged, spurned the ground, and rose again with a roar; and the creeping sea rushed down.

One has the notion that for Flight Commander Raffleton, as for the rest of us, there lies in wait to test the heart of him the ugly and the commonplace. So large a portion of the years will be for him a business of mean hopes and fears, of sordid struggle, of low cares and vulgar fret. But also one has the conviction that there will always remain with him, to make life wonderful, the memory of that night when, godlike, he rode upon the winds of heaven crowned with the glory of the world's desire. Now and again he turned his head to look at her, and still, as ever, her eyes answered him with that strange deep content that seemed to wrap them both around as with a garment of immortality. One gathers dimly something of what he felt from the look that would unconsciously come into his eyes when speaking of that enchanted journey, from the sudden dumbness with which the commonplace words would die away upon his lips. Well for him that his lesser self kept firm hold upon the wheel or maybe a few broken spars, tossing upon the waves, would have been all that was left to tell of a promising young aviator who, on a summer night of June, had thought he could reach the stars.

Half-way across the dawn came flaming up over the Needles, and later there stole from east to west a long, low line of mist-enshrouded land. One by one headland and cliff, flashing with gold, rose out of the sea, and the white-winged gulls flew out to meet them. Almost he expected them to turn into spirits, circling round Malvina with cries of welcome.

Nearer and nearer they drew, while gradually the mist rose upward as the moonlight grew fainter. And all at once the sweep of the Chesil Bank stood out before them, with Weymouth sheltering behind it.

It may have been the bathing-machines, or the gasometer beyond the railway station, or the flag above the Royal Hotel. The curtains of the night fell suddenly away from him. The workaday world came knocking at the door.

He looked at his watch. It was a little after four. He had wired them at the camp to expect him in the morning. They would be looking out for him. By continuing his course he and Malvina could be there about breakfast-time. He could introduce her to the colonel: "Allow me, Colonel Goodyer, the fairy Malvina." It was either that or dropping Malvina somewhere between Weymouth and Farnborough. He decided, without much consideration, that this latter course would be preferable. But where? What was he to do with her? There was Aunt Emily. Hadn't she said something about wanting a French governess for Georgina? True, Malvina's French was a trifle old-fashioned in form, but her accent was charming. And as for salary—There presented itself the thought of Uncle Felix and the three elder boys. Instinctively he felt that Malvina would not be Aunt Emily's idea. His father, had the dear old gentleman been alive, would have been a safe refuge. They had always understood one another, he and his father. But his mother! He was not at all sure. He visualised the scene: the drawing-room at Chester Terrace. His mother's soft, rustling entrance. Her affectionate but well-bred greeting. And then the disconcerting silence with which she would await his explanation of Malvina. The fact that she was a fairy he would probably omit to mention. Faced by his mother's gold-rimmed pince-nez, he did not see himself insisting upon that detail: "A young lady I happened to find asleep on a moor in Brittany. And seeing it was a fine night, and there being just room in the machine. And she—I mean I—well, here we are." There would follow such a painful silence, and then the raising of the delicately arched eyebrows: "You mean, my dear lad, that you have allowed this"—there would be a slight hesitation here—"this young person to leave her home, her people, her friends and relations in Brittany, in order to attach herself to you. May I ask in what capacity?"

For that was precisely how it would look, and not only to his mother. Suppose by a miracle it really represented the facts. Suppose that, in spite of the overwhelming evidence in her favour—of the night and the moon and the stars, and the feeling that had come to him from the moment he had kissed her—suppose that, in spite of all this, it turned out that she wasn't a fairy. Suppose that suggestion of vulgar Common Sense, that she was just a little minx that had run away from home, had really hit the mark. Suppose inquiries were already on foot. A hundred horse-power aeroplane does not go about unnoticed. Wasn't there a law about this sort of thing—something about "decoying" and "young girls"? He hadn't "decoyed" her. If anything, it was the other way about. But would her consent be a valid defence? How old was she? That would be the question. In reality he supposed about a thousand years or so. Possibly more. Unfortunately, she didn't look it. A coldly suspicious magistrate would probably consider sixteen a much better guess. Quite possibly he was going to get into a devil of a mess over this business. He cast a glance behind him. Malvina responded with her changeless smile of ineffable content. For the first time it caused him a distinct feeling of irritation.

They were almost over Weymouth by this time. He could read plainly the advertisement posters outside the cinema theatre facing the esplanade: "Wilkins and the Mermaid. Comic Drama." There was a picture of the lady combing her hair; also of Wilkins, a stoutish gentleman in striped bathing costume.

That mad impulse that had come to him with the first breath of dawn, to shake the dwindling world from his pinions, to plunge upward towards the stars never to return—he wished to Heaven he had yielded to it.

And then suddenly there leapt to him the thought of Cousin Christopher.

Dear old Cousin Christopher, fifty-eight and a bachelor. Why had it not occurred to him before? Out of the sky there appeared to Commander Raffleton the vision of "Cousin Christopher" as a plump, rubicund angel in a panama hat and a pepper-and-salt tweed suit holding out a lifebelt. Cousin Christopher would take to Malvina as some motherly hen to an orphaned duckling. A fairy discovered asleep beside one of the ancient menhirs of Brittany. His only fear would be that you might want to take her away before he had written a paper about her. He would be down from Oxford at his cottage. Commander Raffleton could not for the moment remember the name of the village. It would come to him. It was northwest of Newbury. You crossed Salisbury Plain and made straight for Magdalen Tower. The Downs reached almost to the orchard gate. There was a level stretch of sward nearly half a mile long. It seemed to Commander Raffleton that Cousin Christopher had been created and carefully preserved by Providence for this particular job.

He was no longer the moonstruck youth of the previous night, on whom phantasy and imagination could play what pranks they chose. That part of him the keen, fresh morning air had driven back into its cell. He was Commander Raffleton, an eager and alert young engineer with all his wits about him. At this point that has to be remembered. Descending on a lonely reach of shore he proceeded to again disturb Malvina for the purpose of extracting tins. He expected his passenger would in broad daylight prove to be a pretty, childish-looking girl, somewhat dishevelled, with, maybe, a tinge of blue about the nose, the natural result of a three-hours' flight at fifty miles an hour. It was with a startling return of his original sensations when first she had come to life beneath his kiss that he halted a few feet away and stared at her. The night was gone, and the silence. She stood there facing the sunlight, clad in a Burberry overcoat half a dozen sizes too large for her. Beyond her was a row of bathing-machines, and beyond that again a gasometer. A goods train half a mile away was noisily shunting trucks.

And yet the glamour was about her still; something indescribable but quite palpable—something out of which she looked at you as from another world.

He took her proffered hand, and she leapt out lightly. She was not in the least dishevelled. It seemed as if the air must be her proper element. She looked about her, interested, but not curious. Her first thought was for the machine.

"Poor thing!" she said. "He must be tired."

That faint tremor of fear that had come to him when beneath the menhir's shadow he had watched the opening of her eyes, returned to him. It was not an unpleasant sensation. Rather it added a piquancy to their relationship. But it was distinctly real. She watched the feeding of the monster; and then he came again and stood beside her on the yellow sands.

"England!" he explained with a wave of his hand. One fancies she had the impression that it belonged to him. Graciously she repeated the name. And somehow, as it fell from her lips, it conjured up to Commander Raffleton a land of wonder and romance.

"I have heard of it," she added. "I think I shall like it."

He answered that he hoped she would. He was deadly serious about it. He possessed, generally speaking, a sense of humour; but for the moment this must have deserted him. He told her he was going to leave her in the care of a wise and learned man called "Cousin Christopher"; his description no doubt suggesting to Malvina a friendly magician. He himself would have to go away for a little while, but would return.

It did not seem to matter to Malvina, these minor details. It was evident—the idea in her mind—that he had been appointed to her. Whether as master or servant it was less easy to conjecture: probably a mixture of both, with preference towards the latter.

He mentioned again that he would not be away for longer than he could help. There was no necessity for this repetition. She wasn't doubting it.

Weymouth with its bathing machines and its gasometer faded away. King Rufus was out a-hunting as they passed over the New Forest, and from Salisbury Plain, as they looked down, the pixies waved their hands and laughed. Later, they heard the clang of the anvil, telling them they were in the neighbourhood of Wayland Smith's cave; and so planed down sweetly and without a jar just beyond Cousin Christopher's orchard gate.

A shepherd's boy was whistling somewhere upon the Downs, and in the valley a ploughman had just harnessed his team; but the village was hidden from them by the sweep of the hills, and no other being was in sight. He helped Malvina out, and leaving her seated on a fallen branch beneath a walnut tree, proceeded cautiously towards the house. He found a little maid in the garden. She had run out of the house on hearing the sound of his propeller and was staring up into the sky, so that she never saw him until he put his hand upon her shoulder, and then was fortunately too frightened to scream. He gave her hasty instructions. She was to knock at the Professor's door and tell him that his cousin, Commander Raffleton, was there, and would he come down at once, by himself, into the orchard. Commander Raffleton would rather not come in. Would the Professor come down at once and speak to Commander Raffleton in the orchard.

She went back into the house, repeating it all to herself, a little scared.

"Good God!" said Cousin Christopher from beneath the bedclothes. "He isn't hurt, is he?"

The little maid, through the jar of the door, thought not. Anyhow, he didn't look it. But would the Professor kindly come at once? Commander Raffleton was waiting for him—in the orchard.

So Cousin Christopher, in bedroom slippers, without socks, wearing a mustard-coloured dressing-gown and a black skull cap upon his head—the very picture of a friendly magician—trotted hastily downstairs and through the garden, talking to himself about "foolhardy boys" and "knowing it would happen"; and was much relieved to meet young Arthur Raffleton coming towards him, evidently sound in wind and limb. And then began to wonder why the devil he had been frightened out of bed at six o'clock in the morning if nothing was the matter.

But something clearly was. Before speaking Arthur Raffleton looked carefully about him in a manner suggestive of mystery, if not of crime; and still without a word, taking Cousin Christopher by the arm, led the way to the farther end of the orchard. And there, on a fallen branch beneath the walnut tree, Cousin Christopher saw apparently a khaki coat, with nothing in it, which, as they approached it, rose up.

But it did not rise very high. The back of the coat was towards them. Its collar stood out against the sky line. But there wasn't any head. Standing upright, it turned round, and peeping out of its folds Cousin Christopher saw a child's face. And then looking closer saw that it wasn't a child. And then wasn't quite sure what it was; so that coming to a sudden halt in front of it, Cousin Christopher stared at it with round wide eyes, and then at Flight Commander Raffleton.

It was to Malvina that Flight Commander Raffleton addressed himself.

"This," he said, "is Professor Littlecherry, my Cousin Christopher, about whom I told you."

It was obvious that Malvina regarded the Professor as a person of importance. Evidently her intention was to curtsy, an operation that, hampered by those trailing yards of clinging khaki, might prove—so it flashed upon the Professor—not only difficult but dangerous.

"Allow me," said the Professor.

His idea was to help Malvina out of Commander Raffleton's coat, and Malvina was preparing to assist him. Commander Raffleton was only just in time.

"I don't think," said Commander Raffleton. "If you don't mind I think we'd better leave that for Mrs. Muldoon."

The Professor let go the coat. Malvina appeared a shade disappointed. One opines that not unreasonably she may have thought to make a better impression without it. But a smiling acquiescence in all arrangements made for her welfare seems to have been one of her charms.

"Perhaps," suggested Commander Raffleton to Malvina while refastening a few of the more important buttons, "if you wouldn't mind explaining yourself to my Cousin Christopher just exactly who and what you are—you'd do it so much better than I should." (What Commander Raffleton was saying to himself was: "If I tell the dear old Johnny, he'll think I'm pulling his leg. It will sound altogether different the way she will put it.") "You're sure you don't mind?"

Malvina hadn't the slightest objection. She accomplished her curtsy—or rather it looked as if the coat were curtsying—quite gracefully, and with a dignity one would not have expected from it.

"I am the fairy Malvina," she explained to the Professor. "You may have heard of me. I was the favourite of Harbundia, Queen of the White Ladies of Brittany. But that was long ago."

The friendly magician was staring at her with a pair of round eyes that in spite of their amazement looked kindly and understanding. They probably encouraged Malvina to complete the confession of her sad brief history.

"It was when King Heremon ruled over Ireland," she continued. "I did a very foolish and a wicked thing, and was punished for it by being cast out from the companionship of my fellows. Since then"—the coat made the slightest of pathetic gestures—"I have wandered alone."

It ought to have sounded so ridiculous to them both; told on English soil in the year One Thousand Nine Hundred and Fourteen to a smart young officer of Engineers and an elderly Oxford Professor. Across the road the doctor's odd man was opening garage doors; a noisy milk cart was clattering through the village a little late for the London train; a faint odour of eggs and bacon came wafted through the garden, mingled with the scent of lavender and pinks. For Commander Raffleton, maybe, there was excuse. This story, so far as it has gone, has tried to make that clear. But the Professor! He ought to have exploded in a burst of Homeric laughter, or else to have shaken his head at her and warned her where little girls go to who do this sort of thing.

Instead of which he stared from Commander Raffleton to Malvina, and from Malvina back to Commander Raffleton with eyes so astonishingly round that they might have been drawn with a compass.

"God bless my soul!" said the Professor. "But this is most extraordinary!"

"Was there a King Heremon of Ireland?" asked Commander Raffleton. The Professor was a well-known authority on these matters.

"Of course there was a King Heremon of Ireland," answered the Professor quite petulantly—as if the Commander had wanted to know if there had ever been a Julius Caesar or a Napoleon. "And so there was a Queen Harbundia. Malvina is always spoken of in connection with her."

"What did she do?" inquired Commander Raffleton. They both of them seemed to be oblivious of Malvina's presence.

"I forget for the moment," confessed the professor. "I must look it up. Something, if I remember rightly, in connection with the daughter of King Dancrat. He founded the Norman dynasty. William the Conqueror and all that lot. Good Lord!"

"Would you mind her staying with you for a time until I can make arrangements," suggested Commander Raffleton. "I'd be awfully obliged if you would."

What the Professor's answer might have been had he been allowed to exercise such stock of wits as he possessed, it is impossible to say. Of course he was interested—excited, if you will. Folklore, legend, tradition; these had been his lifelong hobbies. Apart from anything else, here at least was a kindred spirit. Seemed to know a thing or two. Where had she learned it? Might not there be sources unknown to the Professor?

But to take her in! To establish her in the only spare bedroom. To introduce her—as what? to English village society. To the new people at the Manor House. To the member of Parliament with his innocent young wife who had taken the vicarage for the summer. To Dawson, R.A., and the Calthorpes!

He might, had he thought it worth his while, have found some respectable French family and boarded her out. There was a man he had known for years at Oxford, a cabinetmaker; the wife a most worthy woman. He could have gone over there from time to time, his notebook in his pocket, and have interviewed her.

Left to himself, he might have behaved as a sane and rational citizen; or he might not. There are records favouring the latter possibility. The thing is not certain. But as regards this particular incident in his career he must be held exonerated. The decision was taken out of his hands.

To Malvina, on first landing in England, Commander Raffleton had stated his intention of leaving her temporarily in the care of the wise and learned Christopher. To Malvina, regarding the Commander as a gift from the gods, that had settled the matter. The wise and learned Christopher, of course, knew of this coming. In all probability it was he—under the guidance of the gods—who had arranged the whole sequence of events. There remained only to tender him her gratitude. She did not wait for the Professor's reply. The coat a little hindered her but, on the other hand, added perhaps an appealing touch of its own. Taking the wise and learned Christopher's hand in both her own, she knelt and kissed it.

And in that quaint archaic French of hers, that long study of the Chronicles of Froissart enabled the Professor to understand:

"I thank you," she said, "for your noble courtesy and hospitality."

In some mysterious way the whole affair had suddenly become imbued with the dignity of an historical event. The Professor had the sudden impression—and indeed it never altogether left him so long as Malvina remained—that he was a great and powerful personage. A sister potentate; incidentally—though, of course, in high politics such points are immaterial—the most bewilderingly beautiful being he had ever seen; had graciously consented to become his guest. The Professor, with a bow that might have been acquired at the court of King Rene, expressed his sense of the honour done to him. What else could a self-respecting potentate do? The incident was closed.

Flight Commander Raffleton seems to have done nothing in the direction of re-opening it. On the contrary, he appears to have used this precise moment for explaining to the Professor how absolutely necessary it was that he should depart for Farnborough without another moment's loss of time. Commander Raffleton added that he would "look them both up again" the first afternoon he could get away; and was sure that if the Professor would get Malvina to speak slowly, he would soon find her French easy to understand.

It did occur to the Professor to ask Commander Raffleton where he had found Malvina—that is, if he remembered. Also what he was going to do about her—that is, if he happened to know. Commander Raffleton, regretting his great need of haste, explained that he had found Malvina asleep beside a menhir not far from Huelgoat, in Brittany, and was afraid that he had woke her up. For further particulars, would the Professor kindly apply to Malvina? For himself, he would never, he felt sure, be able to thank the professor sufficiently.

In conclusion, and without giving further opportunity for discussion, the Commander seems to have shaken his Cousin Christopher by the hand with much enthusiasm; and then to have turned to Malvina. She did not move, but her eyes were fixed on him. And he came to her slowly. And without a word he kissed her full upon the lips.

"That is twice you have kissed me," said Malvina—and a curious little smile played round her mouth. "The third time I shall become a woman."

4——How It Was Kept from Mrs. Arlington

What surprised the Professor himself, when he came to think of it, was that, left alone with Malvina, and in spite of all the circumstances, he felt neither embarrassment nor perplexity. It was as if, so far as they two were concerned, the whole thing was quite simple—almost humorous. It would be the other people who would have to worry.

The little serving maid was hovering about the garden. She was evidently curious and trying to get a peep. Mrs. Muldoon's voice could be heard calling to her from the kitchen. There was this question of clothes.

"You haven't brought anything with you?" asked the Professor. "I mean, in the way of a frock of any sort."

Malvina, with a smile, gave a little gesture. It implied that all there was of her and hers stood before him.

"We shall have to find you something," said the Professor. "Something in which you can go about—"

The Professor had intended to say "our world," but hesitated, not feeling positive at the moment to which he himself belonged; Malvina's or Mrs. Muldoon's. So he made it "the" world instead. Another gesture conveyed to him that Malvina was entirely in his hands.

"What really have you got on?" asked the Professor. "I mean underneath. Is it anything possible—for a day or two?"

Now Commander Raffleton, for some reason of his own not at all clear to Malvina, had forbidden the taking off of the coat. But had said nothing about undoing it. So by way of response Malvina undid it.

Upon which the Professor, to Malvina's surprise, acted precisely as Commander Raffleton had done. That is to say, he hastily re-closed the coat, returning the buttons to their buttonholes.

The fear may have come to Malvina that she was doomed never to be rid of Commander Raffleton's coat.

"I wonder," mused the Professor, "if anyone in the village—" The little serving maid flittering among the gooseberry bushes—she was pretending to be gathering goose-berries—caught the Professor's eye.

"We will consult my chatelaine, Mrs. Muldoon," suggested the Professor. "I think we shall be able to manage."

The Professor tendered Malvina his arm. With her other hand she gathered up the skirts of the Commander's coat.

"I think," said the Professor with a sudden inspiration as they passed through the garden, "I think I shall explain to Mrs. Muldoon that you have just come straight from a fancy-dress ball."

They found Mrs. Muldoon in the kitchen. A less convincing story than that by which the Professor sought to account to Mrs. Muldoon for the how and the why of Malvina it would be impossible to imagine. Mrs. Muldoon out of sheer kindness appears to have cut him short.

"I'll not be asking ye any questions," said Mrs. Muldoon, "so there'll be no need for ye to imperil your immortal soul. If ye'll just give a thought to your own appearance and leave the colleen to me and Drusilla, we'll make her maybe a bit dacent.

The reference to his own appearance disconcerted the Professor. He had not anticipated, when hastening into his dressing gown and slippers and not bothering about his socks, that he was on his way to meet the chief lady-in-waiting of Queen Harbundia. Demanding that shaving water should be immediately sent up to him, he appears to have retired into the bathroom.

It was while he was shaving that Mrs. Muldoon, knocking at the door, demanded to speak to him. From her tone the Professor came to the conclusion that the house was on fire. He opened the door, and Mrs. Muldoon, seeing he was respectable, slipped in and closed it behind her.

"Where did ye find her? How did she get here?" demanded Mrs. Muldoon. Never before had the Professor seen Mrs. Muldoon other than a placid, good-humoured body. She was trembling from head to foot.

"I told you," explained the Professor. "Young Arthur—"

"I'm not asking ye what ye told me," interrupted Mrs. Muldoon. "I'm asking ye for the truth, if ye know it."

The Professor put a chair for Mrs. Muldoon, and Mrs. Muldoon dropped down upon it.

"What's the matter?" questioned the Professor. "What's happened?"

Mrs. Muldoon glanced round her, and her voice was an hysterical whisper.

"It's no mortal woman ye've brought into the house," said Mrs. Muldoon. "It's a fairy."

Whether up to that moment the Professor had really believed Malvina's story, or whether lurking at the back of his mind there had all along been an innate conviction that the thing was absurd, the Professor himself is now unable to say. To the front of the Professor lay Oxford— political economy, the higher criticism, the rise and progress of rationalism. Behind him, fading away into the dim horizon of humanity, lay an unmapped land where for forty years he had loved to wander; a spirit-haunted land of buried mysteries, lost pathways, leading unto hidden gates of knowledge.

And now upon the trembling balance descended Mrs. Muldoon plump.

"How do you know?" demanded the Professor.

"Shure, don't I know the mark?" replied Mrs. Muldoon almost contemptuously. "Wasn't my own sister's child stolen away the very day of its birth and in its place—"

The little serving maid tapped at the door.

Mademoiselle was "finished." What was to be done with her?

"Don't ask me," protested Mrs. Muldoon, still in a terrified whisper. "I couldn't do it. Not if all the saints were to go down upon their knees and pray to me."

Common-sense argument would not have prevailed with Mrs. Muldoon. The Professor felt that; added to which he had not any handy. He directed, through the door, that "Mademoiselle" should be shown into the dining-room, and listened till Drusilla's footsteps had died away.

"Have you ever heard of the White Ladies?" whispered the Professor to Mrs. Muldoon.

There was not much in the fairy line, one takes it, that Mrs. Muldoon had not heard of and believed. Was the Professor sure?

The Professor gave Mrs. Muldoon his word of honour as a gentleman. The "White Ladies," as Mrs. Muldoon was of course aware, belonged to the "good people." Provided nobody offended her there was nothing to fear.

"Shure, it won't be meself that'll cross her," said Mrs. Muldoon.

"She won't be staying very long," added the Professor. "We will just be nice to her."

"She's got a kind face," admitted Mrs. Muldoon, "and a pleasant way with her." The good body's spirits were perceptibly rising. The favour of a "White Lady" might be worth cultivating.

"We must make a friend of her," urged the Professor, seizing his opportunity.

"And mind," whispered the Professor as he opened the door for Mrs. Muldoon to slip out, "not a word. She doesn't want it known."

One is convinced that Mrs. Muldoon left the bathroom resolved that, so far as she could help it, no breath of suspicion that Malvina was other than what in Drusilla's holiday frock she would appear to be should escape into the village. It was quite a pleasant little frock of a summery character, with short sleeves and loose about the neck, and fitted Malvina, in every sense, much better than the most elaborate confection would have done. The boots were not so successful. Malvina solved the problem by leaving them behind her, together with the stockings, whenever she went out. That she knew this was wrong is proved by the fact that invariably she tried to hide them. They would be found in the most unlikely places; hidden behind books in the Professor's study, crammed into empty tea canisters in Mrs. Muldoon's storeroom. Mrs. Muldoon was not to be persuaded even to abstract them. The canister with its contents would be placed in silence upon the Professor's table. Malvina on returning would be confronted by a pair of stern, unsympathetic boots. The corners of the fairy mouth would droop in lines suggestive of penitence and contrition.

Had the Professor been firm she would have yielded. But from the black accusing boots the Professor could not keep his eyes from wandering to the guilty white feet, and at once in his heart becoming "counsel for the defence." Must get a pair of sandals next time he went to Oxford. Anyhow, something more dainty than those grim, uncompromising boots.

Besides, it was not often that Malvina ventured beyond the orchard. At least not during the day time—perhaps one ought to say not during that part of the day time when the village was astir. For Malvina appears to have been an early riser. Somewhere about the middle of the night, as any Christian body would have timed it, Mrs. Muldoon—waking and sleeping during this period in a state of high nervous tension—would hear the sound of a softly opened door; peeping from a raised corner of the blind, would catch a glimpse of fluttering garments that seemed to melt into the dawn; would hear coming fainter and fainter from the uplands an unknown song, mingling with the answering voices of the birds.

It was on the uplands between dawn and sunrise that Malvina made the acquaintance of the Arlington twins.

They ought, of course, to have been in bed—all three of them, for the matter of that. The excuse for the twins was their Uncle George. He had been telling them all about the Uffington spectre and Wayland Smith's cave, and had given them "Puck" as a birthday present. They were always given their birthday presents between them, because otherwise they did not care for them. They had retired to their respective

29

bedrooms at ten o'clock and taken it in turns to lie awake. At the first streak of dawn Victoria, who had been watching by her window, woke Victor, as arranged. Victor was for giving it up and going to sleep again, but Victoria reminding him of the "oath," they dressed themselves quite simply, and let themselves down by the ivy.

They came across Malvina close to the tail of the White Horse. They knew she was a fairy the moment they saw her. But they were not frightened—at least not very much. It was Victor who spoke first. Taking off his hat and going down on one knee, he wished Malvina good morning and hoped she was quite well. Malvina, who seemed pleased to see them, made answer, and here it was that Victoria took charge of the affair. The Arlington twins until they were nine had shared a French nurse between them; and then Victor, going to school, had gradually forgotten; while Victoria, remaining at home, had continued her conversations with "madame."

"Oh!" said Victoria. "Then you must be a French fairy."

Now the Professor had impressed upon Malvina that for reasons needless to be explained—anyhow, he never had explained them—she was not to mention that she was a fairy. But he had not told her to deny it. Indeed how could she? The most that could be expected from her was that she should maintain silence on the point. So in answer to Victoria she explained that her name was Malvina, and that she had flown across from Brittany in company with "Sir Arthur," adding that she had often heard of England and had wished to see it.

"How do you like it?" demanded Victoria.

Malvina confessed herself charmed with it. Nowhere had she ever met so many birds. Malvina raised her hand and they all three stood in silence, listening. The sky was ablaze and the air seemed filled with their music. The twins were sure that there were millions of them. They must have come from miles and miles and miles, to sing to Malvina.

Also the people. They were so good and kind and round. Malvina for the present was staying with—accepting the protection, was how she put it, of the wise and learned Christopher. The "habitation" could be seen from where they stood, its chimneys peeping from among the trees. The twins exchanged a meaning glance. Had they not all along suspected the Professor! His black skull cap, and his big hooked nose, and the yellow-leaved, worm-eaten books—of magic: all doubts were now removed—that for hours he would sit poring over through owlish gold-rimmed spectacles!

Victor's French was coming back to him. He was anxious to know if Malvina had ever met Sir Launcelot—"to talk to."

A little cloud gathered upon Malvina's face. Yes, she had known them all: King Uthur and Igraine and Sir Ulfias of the Isles. Talked with them, walked with them in the fair lands of France. (It ought to have been England, but Malvina shook her head. Maybe they had travelled.) It was she who had saved Sir Tristram from the wiles of Morgan le Fay. "Though that, of course," explained Malvina, "was never known."

The twins were curious why it should have been "of course," but did not like to interrupt again. There were others before and after. Most of them the twins had never heard of until they came to Charlemagne, beyond which Malvina's reminiscences appeared to fade.

They had all of them been very courteous to her, and some of them indeed quite charming. But . . .

One gathers they had never been to Malvina more than mere acquaintances, such as one passes the time with while waiting—and longing.

"But you liked Sir Launcelot," urged Victor. He was wishful that Malvina should admire Sir Launcelot, feeling how much there was in common between that early lamented knight and himself. That little affair with Sir Bedivere. It was just how he would have behaved himself.

Ah! yes, admitted Malvina. She had "liked" him. He was always so—so "excellent."

"But he was not—none of them were my own people, my own dear companions." The little cloud had settled down again.

It was Bruno who recalled the three of them to the period of contemporary history.

Polley the cowman's first duty in the morning was to let Bruno loose for a run. He arrived panting and breathless, and evidently offended at not having been included in the escapade. He could have given them both away quite easily if he had not been the most forgiving of black-and-tan collies. As it was, he had been worrying himself crazy for the last half-hour, feeling sure they had forgotten the time. "Don't you know it's nearly six o'clock? That in less than half an hour Jane will be knocking at your doors with glasses of hot milk, and will probably drop them and scream when she finds your beds empty and the window wide open." That is what he had intended should be his first words, but on scenting Malvina they went from him entirely. He gave her one look and flopped down flat, wriggling towards her, whining and wagging his tail at the same time. Malvina acknowledged his homage by laughing and patting his head with her foot, and that sent him into the seventh heaven of delight. They all four descended the hill together and parted at the orchard gate. The twins expressed a polite but quite sincere hope that they would have the pleasure of seeing Malvina again; but Malvina, seized maybe with sudden doubts as to whether she had behaved with discretion, appears to have replied evasively. Ten minutes later she was lying asleep, the golden head pillowed on the round white arm; as Mrs. Muldoon on her way down to the kitchen saw for herself. And the twins, fortunate enough to find a side door open, slipped into the house unnoticed and scrambled back into their beds.

It was quarter past nine when Mrs. Arlington came in herself and woke them up. She was short-tempered with them both and had evidently been crying. They had their breakfast in the kitchen.

During lunch hardly a word was spoken. And there was no pudding. Mr. Arlington, a stout, florid gentleman, had no time for pudding. The rest might sit and enjoy it at their leisure, but not so Mr. Arlington. Somebody had to see to things—that is, if they were not to be allowed to go to rack and ruin. If other people could not be relied upon to do their duty, so that everything inside the house and out of it was thrown upon one pair of shoulders, then it followed as a natural consequence that that pair of shoulders could not spare the necessary time to properly finish its meals. This it was that was at the root of the decay of English farming. When farmers' wives, to say nothing of sons and daughters old enough one might imagine to be anxious to do something in repayment for the money and care lavished upon them, had all put their shoulders to the wheel, then English farming had prospered. When, on the other hand, other people shirked their fair share of labour and responsibility, leaving to one pair of hands.

It was the eldest Arlington girl's quite audible remark that pa could have eaten two helpings of pudding while he had been talking, that caused Mr. Arlington to lose the thread of his discourse. To put it quite bluntly, what Mr. Arlington meant to say was this: He had never wanted to be a farmer—at least not in the beginning. Other men in his position, having acquired competency by years of self-sacrificing labour, would have retired to a well-earned leisure. Having yielded to persuasion and taken on the job, he was going to see it through; and everybody else was going to do their share or there would be trouble.

Mr. Arlington, swallowing the remains of his glass in a single gulp, spoilt a dignified exit by violently hiccoughing, and Mrs. Arlington rang the bell furiously for the parlourmaid to clear away. The pudding passed untouched from before the very eyes of the twins. It was a black-currant pudding with brown sugar.

That night Mrs. Arlington appears to have confided in the twins, partly for her own relief and partly for their moral benefit. If Mrs. Arlington had enjoyed the blessing in disguise of a less indulgent mother, all might have been well. By nature Mrs. Arlington had been endowed with an active and energetic temperament. "Miss Can't-sit-still-a-minute," her nurse had always called her. Unfortunately it had been allowed to sink into disuse; was now in all probability beyond hope of recovery. Their father was quite right. When they had lived in Bayswater and the business was in Mincing Lane it did not matter. Now it was different. A farmer's wife ought to be up at six; she ought to see that everybody else was up at six; servants looked after, kept up to the mark; children encouraged by their mother's example. Organisation. That was what was wanted. The day mapped out; to every hour its appointed task. Then, instead of the morning being gone before you could turn yourself round, and confusion made worse confounded by your leaving off what you were doing and trying to do six things at once that you couldn't remember whether you had done or whether you hadn't . . .

Here Mrs. Arlington appears to have dissolved into tears. Generally speaking, she was a placid, smiling, most amiable lady, quite delightful to have about the house provided all you demanded of her were pleasant looks and a sunny disposition. The twins appear to have joined their tears to hers. Tucked in and left to themselves, one imagines the problem being discussed with grave seriousness, much whispered conversation, then slept upon, the morning bringing with it ideas. The result being that the next evening, between high tea and supper, Mrs. Muldoon, answering herself the knock at the door, found twin figures standing hand in hand on the Professor's step.

They asked her if "the Fairy" was in.

5—How It Was Told to Mrs. Marigold

There was no need of the proverbial feather. Mrs. Muldoon made a grab at the settle but missed it. She caught at a chair, but that gave way. It was the floor that finally stopped her.

"We're so sorry," apologised Victor. "We thought you knew. We ought to have said Mademoiselle Malvina."

Mrs. Muldoon regained her feet, and without answering walked straight into the study.

"They want to know," said Mrs. Muldoon, "if the Fairy's in." The Professor, with his back to the window, was reading. The light in the room was somewhat faint.

"Who wants to know?" demanded the Professor.

"The twins from the Manor House," explained Mrs. Muldoon.

"But what?—but who?" began the Professor.

"Shall I say 'not at home'?" suggested Mrs. Muldoon. "Or hadn't you better see them yourself."

"Show them in," directed the Professor.

They came in, looking a little scared and still holding one another by the hand. They wished the Professor good evening, and when he rose they backed away from him. The Professor shook hands with them, but they did not let go, so that Victoria gave him her right hand and Victor his left, and then at the Professor's invitation they sat themselves down on the extreme edge of the sofa.

"I hope we do not disturb you," said Victor. "We wanted to see Mademoiselle Malvina."

"Why do you want to see Mademoiselle Malvina?" inquired the Professor.

"It is something very private," said Victor.

"We wanted to ask her a great favour," said Victoria.

"I'm sorry," said the Professor, "but she isn't in. At least, I don't think so." (The Professor never was quite sure. "She slips in and out making no more noise than a wind-driven rose leaf," was Mrs. Muldoon's explanation.) "Hadn't you better tell me? Leave me to put it to her."

They looked at one another. It would never do to offend the wise and learned Christopher. Besides, a magician, it is to be assumed, has more ways than one of learning what people are thinking.

"It is about mamma," explained Victoria. "We wondered if Malvina would mind changing her."

The Professor had been reading up Malvina. It flashed across him that this had always been her speciality: Changing people. How had the Arlington twins discovered it? And why did they want their mother changed? And what did they want her changed into? It was shocking when you come to think of it! The Professor became suddenly so stern, that if the twins could have seen his expression—which, owing to the fading light, they couldn't—they would have been too frightened to answer.

"Why do you want your mother changed?" demanded the Professor. Even as it was his voice alarmed them.

"It's for her own good," faltered Victoria.

"Of course we don't mean into anything," explained Victor.

"Only her inside," added Victoria.

"We thought that Malvina might be able to improve her," completed Victor.

It was still very disgraceful. What were we coming to when children went about clamouring for their mothers to be "improved"! The atmosphere was charged with indignation. The twins felt it.

"She wants to be," persisted Victoria. "She wants to be energetic and to get up early in the morning and do things."

"You see," added Victor, "she was never properly brought up."

The Professor maintains stoutly that his only intention was a joke. It was not even as if anything objectionable had been suggested. The Professor himself had on occasions been made the confidant of both.

"Best woman that ever lived, if only one could graft a little energy upon her. No sense of time. Too easy-going. No idea of keeping people up to the mark." So Mr. Arlington, over the nuts and wine.

"It's pure laziness. Oh, yes, it is. My friends say I'm so 'restful'; but that's the proper explanation of it—born laziness. And yet I try. You have no idea, Professor Littlecherry, how much I try." So Mrs. Arlington, laughingly, while admiring the Professor's roses.

Besides, how absurd to believe that Malvina could possibly change anybody! Way back, when the human brain was yet in process of evolution, such things may have been possible. Hypnotic suggestion, mesmeric influence, dormant brain cells quickened into activity by magnetic vibration. All that had been lost. These were the days of George the Fifth, not of King Heremon. What the Professor was really after was: How would Malvina receive the proposal? Of course she would try to get out of it. A dear little thing. But could any sane man, professor of mathematics . . .

Malvina was standing beside him. No one had remarked her entrance. The eyes of the twins had been glued upon the wise and learned Christopher. The Professor, when he was thinking, never saw anything. Still, it was rather startling.

"We should never change what the good God has once fashioned," said Malvina. She spoke very gravely. The childishness seemed to have fallen from her.

"You didn't always think so," said the Professor. It nettled the Professor that all idea of this being a good joke had departed with the sound of Malvina's voice. She had that way with her.

She made a little gesture. It conveyed to the Professor that his remark had not been altogether in good taste.

"I speak as one who has learned," said Malvina.

"I beg your pardon," said the Professor. "I ought not to have said that."

Malvina accepted the Professor's apology with a bow.

"But this is something very different," continued the Professor. Quite another interest had taken hold of the Professor. It was easy enough to summon Dame Commonsense to one's aid when Malvina was not present. Before those strange eyes the good lady had a habit of sneaking away. Suppose—of course the idea was ridiculous, but suppose—something did happen! As a psychological experiment was not one justified? What was the beginning of all science but applied curiosity? Malvina might be able—and willing—to explain how it was done. That is, if anything did happen, which, of course, it wouldn't, and so much the better. This thing had got to be ended.

"It would be using a gift not for one's own purposes, but to help others," urged the Professor.

"You see," urged Victor, "mamma really wants to be changed."

"And papa wants it too," urged Victoria.

"It seems to me, if I may so express it," added the Professor, "that really it would be in the nature of making amends for—well, for—for our youthful follies," concluded the Professor a little nervously.

Malvina's eyes were fixed on the Professor. In the dim light of the low-ceilinged room, those eyes seemed all of her that was visible.

"You wish it?" said Malvina.

It was not at all fair, as the Professor told himself afterwards, her laying the responsibility on him. If she really was the original Malvina, lady-in-waiting to Queen Harbundia, then she was quite old enough to have decided for herself. From the Professor's calculations she must now be about three thousand eight hundred. The Professor himself was not yet sixty; in comparison a mere babe! But Malvina's eyes were compelling.

"Well, it can't do any harm," said the Professor. And Malvina seems to have accepted that as her authority.

"Let her come to the Cross Stones at sundown," directed Malvina.

The Professor saw the twins to the door. For some reason the Professor could not have explained, they all three walked out on tiptoe. Old Mr. Brent, the postman, was passing, and the twins ran after him and each took a hand. Malvina was still standing where the Professor had left her. It was very absurd, but the Professor felt frightened. He went into the kitchen, where it was light and cheerful, and started Mrs. Muldoon on Home Rule. When he returned to the parlour Malvina was gone.

The twins did not talk that night, and decided next morning not to say a word, but just to ask their mother to come for an evening walk with them. The fear was that she might demand reasons. But, quite oddly, she consented without question. It seemed to the twins that it was Mrs. Arlington herself who took the pathway leading past the cave, and when they reached the Cross Stones she sat down and apparently had forgotten their existence. They stole away without her noticing them, but did not quite know what to do with themselves. They ran for half a mile till they came to the wood; there they remained awhile, careful not to venture within; and then they crept back. They found their mother sitting just as they had left her. They thought she was asleep, but her eyes were wide open. They were tremendously relieved, though what they had feared they never knew. They sat down, one on each side of her, and each took a hand, but in spite of her eyes being open, it was quite a time before she seemed conscious of their return. She rose and slowly looked about her, and as she did so the church clock struck nine. She could not at first believe it was so late. Convinced by looking at her watch—there was just light enough for her to see it—she became all at once more angry than the twins had ever known her, and for the first time in their lives they both experienced the sensation of having their ears boxed. Nine o'clock was the proper time for supper and they were half an hour from home, and it was all their fault. It did not take them half an hour. It took them twenty minutes, Mrs. Arlington striding ahead and the twins panting breathless behind her. Mr. Arlington had not yet returned. He came in five minutes afterwards, and Mrs. Arlington told him what she thought of him. It was the shortest supper within the twins' recollection. They found themselves in bed ten minutes in advance of the record. They could hear their mother's voice from the kitchen. A jug of milk had been overlooked and had gone sour. She had given Jane a week's notice before the clock struck ten.

It was from Mr. Arlington that the Professor heard the news. Mr. Arlington could not stop an instant, dinner being at twelve sharp and it wanting but ten minutes to; but seems to have yielded to temptation. The breakfast hour at the Manor Farm was now six a.m., had been so since Thursday; the whole family fully dressed and Mrs. Arlington presiding. If the Professor did not believe it he could come round any morning and see for himself. The Professor appears to have taken Mr. Arlington's word for it. By six-thirty everybody at their job and Mrs. Arlington at hers, consisting chiefly of seeing to it for the rest of the day that everybody was. Lights out at ten and everybody in bed; most of them only too glad to be there. "Quite right; keeps us all up to the mark," was Mr. Arlington's opinion (this was on Saturday). Just what was wanted. Not perhaps for a permanency; and, of course, there were drawbacks. The strenuous life—seeing to it that everybody else leads the strenuous life; it does not go with unmixed amiability. Particularly in the beginning. New-born zeal: must expect it to outrun discretion. Does not do to discourage it. Modifications to be suggested later. Taken all round, Mr. Arlington's view was that the thing must be regarded almost as the answer to a prayer. Mr. Arlington's eyes on their way to higher levels, appear to have been arrested by the church clock. It decided Mr. Arlington to resume his homeward way without further loss of time. At the bend of the lane the Professor, looking back, observed that Mr. Arlington had broken into a trot.

This seems to have been the end of the Professor, regarded as a sane and intelligent member of modern society. He had not been sure at the time, but it was now revealed to him that when he had urged Malvina to test her strength, so to express it, on the unfortunate Mrs. Arlington, it was with the conviction that the result would restore him to his mental equilibrium. That Malvina with a wave of her wand—or whatever the hocus-pocus may have been—would be able to transform the hitherto incorrigibly indolent and easy-going Mrs. Arlington into a sort of feminine Lloyd George, had not really entered into his calculations.

Forgetting his lunch, he must have wandered aimlessly about, not returning home until late in the afternoon. During dinner he appears to have been rather restless and nervous—"jumpy," according to the evidence of the little serving maid. Once he sprang out of his chair as if shot when the little serving maid accidentally let fall a table-spoon; and twice he upset the salt. It was at mealtime that, as a rule, the Professor found his attitude towards Malvina most sceptical. A fairy who could put away quite a respectable cut from the joint, followed by two helpings of pie, does take a bit of believing in. To-night the Professor found no difficulty. The White Ladies had never been averse to accepting mortal hospitality. There must always have been a certain adaptability. Malvina, since that fateful night of her banishment, had, one supposes, passed through varied experiences. For present purposes she had assumed the form of a jeune fille of the twentieth century (anno Domini). An appreciation of Mrs. Muldoon's excellent cooking, together with a glass of light sound claret, would naturally go with it.

One takes it that he could not for a moment get Mrs. Arlington out of his mind. More than once, stealing a covert glance across the table, it seemed to him that Malvina was regarding him with a mocking smile. Some impish spirit it must have been that had prompted him. For thousands of years Malvina had led—at all events so far as was known—a reformed and blameless existence; had subdued and put behind her that fatal passion of hers for change: in other people. What madness to have revived it! And no Queen Harbundia handy now to keep her in check. The Professor had a distinct sensation, while peeling a pear, that he was being turned into a guinea-pig—a curious feeling of shrinking about the legs. So vivid was the impression, that involuntarily the Professor jumped off his chair and ran to look at himself in the mirror over the sideboard. He was not fully relieved even then. It may have been the mirror. It was very old; one of those things with little gilt balls all round it; and it looked to the Professor as if his nose was growing straight out of his face. Malvina, trusting he had not been taken suddenly ill, asked if there was anything she could do for him. He seems to have earnestly begged her not to think of it.

The Professor had taught Malvina cribbage, and usually of an evening they played a hand or two. But to-night the Professor was not in the mood, and Malvina had contented herself with a book. She was particularly fond of the old chroniclers. The Professor had an entire shelf of them, many in the original French. Making believe to be reading himself, he heard Malvina break into a cheerful laugh, and went and looked over her shoulder. She was reading the history of her own encounter with the proprietor of tin mines, an elderly gentleman disliking late hours, whom she had turned into a nightingale. It occurred to the Professor that prior to the Arlington case the recalling of this incident would have brought to her shame and remorse. Now she seemed to think it funny.

"A silly trick," commented the Professor. He spoke quite heatedly. "No one has any right to go about changing people. Muddling up things they don't understand. No right whatever."

Malvina looked up. She gave a little sigh.

"Not for one's own pleasure or revenge," she made answer. Her tone was filled with meekness. It had a touch of self-reproach. "That is very wrong, of course. But changing them for their own good—at least, not changing, improving."

"Little hypocrite!" muttered the Professor to himself. "She's got back a taste for her old tricks, and Lord knows now where she'll stop."

The Professor spent the rest of the evening among his indexes in search of the latest information regarding Queen Harbundia.

Meanwhile the Arlington affair had got about the village. The twins in all probability had been unable to keep their secret. Jane, the dismissed, had looked in to give Mrs. Muldoon her version of Thursday night's scene in the Arlington kitchen, and Mrs. Muldoon, with a sense of things impending, may unconsciously have dropped hints.

The Marigolds met the Arlingtons on Sunday, after morning service, and heard all about it. That is to say, they met Mr. Arlington and the other children; Mrs. Arlington, with the two elder girls, having already attended early communion at seven. Mrs. Marigold was a pretty, fluffy, engaging little woman, ten years younger than her husband. She could not have been altogether a fool, or she would not have known it. Marigold, rising politician, ought, of course, to have married a woman able to help him; but seems to have fallen in love with her a few miles out of Brussels, over a convent wall. Mr. Arlington was not a regular church-goer, but felt on this occasion that he owed it to his Maker. He was still in love with his new wife. But not blindly. Later on a guiding hand might be necessary. But first let the new seed get firmly rooted. Marigold's engagements necessitated his returning to town on Sunday afternoon, and Mrs. Marigold walked part of the way with him to the station. On her way back across the fields she picked up the Arlington twins. Later, she seems to have called in at the cottage and spoken to Mrs. Muldoon about Jane, who, she had heard, was in want of a place. A little before sunset she was seen by the Doctor climbing the path to the Warren. Malvina that evening was missing for dinner. When she returned she seemed pleased with herself.

6——And How It Was Finished Too Soon

S ome days later—it may have been the next week; the exact date appears to have got mislaid—Marigold, M.P., looked in on the Professor. They talked about Tariff Reform, and then Marigold got up and made sure for himself that the door was tight closed.

"You know my wife," he said. "We've been married six years, and there's never been a cloud between us except one. Of course, she's not brainy. That is, at least . . ."

The Professor jumped out of his chair.

"If you take my advice," he said, "you'll leave her alone." He spoke with passion and conviction.

Marigold looked up.

"It's just what I wish to goodness I had done," he answered. "I blame myself entirely."

"So long as we see our own mistakes," said the Professor, "there is hope for us all. You go straight home, young man, and tell her you've changed your mind. Tell her you don't want her with brains. Tell her you like her best without. You get that into her head before anything else happens."

"I've tried to," said Marigold. "She says it's too late. That the light has come to her and she can't help it."

It was the Professor's turn to stare. He had not heard anything of Sunday's transactions. He had been hoping against hope that the Arlington affair would remain a locked secret between himself and the twins, and had done his best to think about everything else.

"She's joined the Fabian Society," continued Marigold gloomily. "They've put her in the nursery. And the W.S.P.U. If it gets about before the next election I'll have to look out for another constituency—that's all."

"How did you hear about her?" asked the Professor.

"I didn't hear about her," answered Marigold. "If I had I mightn't have gone up to town. You think it right," he added, "to—to encourage such people?"

"Who's encouraging her?" demanded the professor. "If fools didn't go about thinking they could improve every other fool but themselves, this sort of thing wouldn't happen. Arlington had an amiable, sweet-tempered wife, and instead of thanking God and keeping quiet about it, he worries her out of her life because she is not the managing woman. Well, now he's got the managing woman. I met him on Wednesday with a bump on his forehead as big as an egg. Says he fell over the mat. It can't be done. You can't have a person changed just as far as you want them changed and there stop. You let 'em alone or you change them altogether, and then they don't know themselves what they're going to turn out. A sensible man in your position would have been only too thankful for a wife who didn't poke her nose into his affairs, and with whom he could get away from his confounded politics. You've been hinting to her about once a month, I expect, what a tragedy it was that you hadn't married a woman with brains. Well, now she's found her brains and is using them. Why shouldn't she belong to the Fabian Society and the W.S.P.U? Shows independence of character. Best thing for you to do is to join them yourself. Then you'll be able to work together."

"I'm sorry," said Marigold rising. "I didn't know you agreed with her."

"Who said I agreed with her?" snapped the Professor. "I'm in a very awkward position."

"I suppose," said Marigold—he was hesitating with the door in his hand—"it wouldn't be of any use my seeing her myself?"

"I believe," said the Professor, "that she is fond of the neighbourhood of the Cross Stones towards sundown. You can choose for yourself, but if I were you I should think twice about it."

"I was wondering," said Marigold, "whether, if I put it to her as a personal favour, she might not be willing to see Edith again and persuade her that she was only joking?"

A light began to break upon the Professor.

"What do you think has happened?" he asked.

"Well," explained Marigold, "I take it that your young foreign friend has met my wife and talked politics to her, and that what has happened is the result. She must be a young person of extraordinary ability; but it would be only losing one convert, and I could make it up to her in—in other ways." He spoke with unconscious pathos. It rather touched the Professor.

"It might mean," said the Professor—"that is, assuming that it can be done at all—Mrs. Marigold's returning to her former self entirely, taking no further interest in politics whatever."

"I should be so very grateful," answered Marigold.

The Professor had mislaid his spectacles, but thinks there was a tear in Marigold's eye.

"I'll do what I can," said the Professor. "Of course, you mustn't count on it. It may be easier to start a woman thinking than to stop her, even for a—" The Professor checked himself just in time. "I'll talk to her," he said; and Marigold gripped his hand and departed.

It was about time he did. The full extent of Malvina's activities during those few midsummer weeks, till the return of Flight Commander Raffleton, will never perhaps be fully revealed. According to the Doctor, the whole business has been grossly exaggerated. There are those who talk as if half the village had been taken to pieces, altered and improved and sent back home again in a mental state unrecognisable by their own mothers. Certain it is that Dawson, R.A., generally described by everybody except his wife as "a lovable little man," and whose only fault was an incurable habit of punning, both in season—if such a period there be—and more often out, suddenly one morning smashed a Dutch interior, fifteen inches by nine, over the astonished head of Mrs. Dawson. It clung round her neck, recalling biblical pictures of the head of John the Baptist, and the frame-work had to be sawn through before she could get it off. As to the story about his having been caught by Mrs. Dawson's aunt kissing the housemaid behind the waterbutt, that, as the Doctor admits, is a bit of bad luck that might have happened to anyone. But whether there was really any evidence connecting him with Dolly Calthorpe's unaccountable missing of the last train home, is of course, a more serious matter. Mrs. Dawson, a handsome, high-spirited woman herself, may have found Dawson, as originally fashioned, trying to the nerves; though even then the question arises: Why have married him? But there is a difference, as Mrs. Dawson has pointed out, between a husband who hasn't enough of the natural man in him and a husband who has a deal too much. It is difficult to regulate these matters.

Altogether, and taking an outside estimate, the Doctor's opinion is that there may have been half a dozen, who, with Malvina's assistance, succeeded in hypnotising themselves into temporary insanity. When Malvina, a little disappointed, but yielding quite sweetly her own judgment to that of the wise and learned Christopher, consented to "restore" them, the explanation was that, having spent their burst of ill-acquired energy, they fell back at the first suggestion to their former selves.

Mrs. Arlington does not agree with the Doctor. She had been trying to reform herself for quite a long time and had miserably failed. There was something about them—it might almost be described as an aroma—that prompted her that evening to take the twins into her confidence; a sort of intuition that in some way they could help her. It remained with her all the next day; and when the twins returned in the evening, in company with the postman, she knew instinctively that they had been about her business. It was this same intuitive desire that drew her to the Downs. She is confident she would have taken that walk to the Cross Stones even if the twins had not proposed it. Indeed, according to her own account, she was not aware that the twins had accompanied her. There was something about the stones; a sense as of a presence. She knew when she reached them that she had arrived at the appointed place; and when there appeared to her—coming from where she could not tell—a diminutive figure that seemed in some mysterious way as if it were clothed merely in the fading light, she remembered distinctly that she was neither surprised nor alarmed. The diminutive lady sat down beside her and took Mrs. Arlington's hands in both her own. She spoke in a strange language, but Mrs. Arlington at the time understood it, though now the meaning of it had passed from her. Mrs. Arlington felt as if her body were being taken away from her. She had a sense of falling, a feeling that she must make some desperate effort to rise again. The strange little lady was helping her, assisting her to make this supreme effort. It was as if ages were passing. She was wrestling with unknown powers. Suddenly she seemed to slip from them. The little lady was holding her up. Clasping each other, they rose and rose and rose. Mrs. Arlington had a firm conviction that she must always be struggling upward, or they would overtake her and drag her down again. When she awoke the little lady had gone, but that feeling remained with her; that passionate acceptance of ceaseless struggle, activity, contention, as now the end and aim of her existence. At first she did not recollect where she was. A strange colourless light was around her, and a strange singing as of myriads of birds. And then the clock struck nine and life came back to her with a rush. But with it still that conviction that she must seize hold of herself and everybody else and get things done. Its immediate expression, as already has been mentioned, was experienced by the twins.

When, after a talk with the Professor, aided and abetted by Mr. Arlington and the eldest Arlington girl, she consented to pay that second visit to the stones, it was with very different sensations that she climbed the grass-grown path. The little lady had met her as before, but the curious deep eyes looked sadly, and Mrs. Arlington had the impression, generally speaking, that she was about to assist at her own funeral. Again the little lady took her by the hands, and again she experienced that terror of falling. But instead of ending with contest and effort she seemed to pass into a sleep, and when she opened her eyes she was again alone. Feeling a little chilly and unreasonably tired, she walked slowly home, and not being hungry, retired supperless to bed. Quite unable to explain why, she seems to have cried herself to sleep.

One supposes that something of a similar nature may have occurred to the others—with the exception of Mrs. Marigold. It was the case of Mrs. Marigold that, as the Doctor grudgingly admits, went far to weaken his hypothesis. Mrs. Marigold, having emerged, was spreading herself, much to her own satisfaction. She had discarded her wedding ring as a relic of barbarism—of the days when women were mere goods and chattels, and had made her first speech at a meeting in favour of marriage reform. Subterfuge, in her case, had to be resorted to. Malvina had tearfully consented, and Marigold, M.P., was to bring Mrs. Marigold to the Cross Stones that same evening and there leave her, explaining to her that Malvina had expressed a wish to see her again—"just for a chat."

All might have ended well if only Commander Raffleton had not appeared framed in the parlour door just as Malvina was starting. His Cousin Christopher had written to the Commander. Indeed, after the Arlington affair, quite pressingly, and once or twice had thought he heard the sound of Flight Commander Raffleton's propeller, but on each occasion had been disappointed. "Affairs of State," Cousin Christopher had explained to Malvina, who, familiar one takes it with the calls upon knights and warriors through all the ages, had approved.

He stood there with his helmet in his hand.

"Only arrived this afternoon from France," he explained. "Haven't a moment to spare."

But he had just time to go straight to Malvina. He laughed as he took her in his arms and kissed her full upon the lips.

When last he had kissed her—it had been in the orchard; the Professor had been witness to it—Malvina had remained quite passive, only that curious little smile about her lips. But now an odd thing happened. A quivering seemed to pass through all her body, so that it swayed and trembled. The Professor feared she was going to fall; and, maybe to save herself, she put up her arms about Commander Raffleton's neck, and with a strange low cry—it sounded to the Professor like the cry one sometimes hears at night from some little dying creature of the woods—she clung to him sobbing.

It must have been a while later when the chiming of the clock recalled to the Professor the appointment with Mrs. Marigold.

"You will only just have time," he said, gently seeking to release her. "I'll promise to keep him till you come back." And as Malvina did not seem to understand, he reminded her.

But still she made no movement, save for a little gesture of the hands as if she were seeking to lay hold of something unseen. And then she dropped her arms and looked from one of them to the other. The Professor did not think of it at the time, but remembered afterwards; that strange aloofness of hers, as if she were looking at you from another world. One no longer felt it.

"I am so sorry," she said. "It is too late. I am only a woman."

And Mrs. Marigold is still thinking.

The Prologue

A nd here follows the Prologue. It ought, of course, to have been written first, but nobody knew of it until quite the end entirely. It was told to Commander Raffleton by a French comrade, who in days of peace had been a painter, mingling with others of his kind, especially such as found their inspiration in the wide horizons and legend-haunted dells of old-world Brittany. Afterwards the Commander told it to the Professor, and the Professor's only stipulation was that it should not be told to the Doctor, at least for a time. For the Doctor would see in it only confirmation for his own narrow sense-bound theories, while to the Professor it confirmed beyond a doubt the absolute truth of this story.

It commenced in the year Eighteen hundred and ninety-eight (anno Domini), on a particularly unpleasant evening in late February—"a stormy winter's night," one would describe it, were one writing mere romance. It came to the lonely cottage of Madame Lavigne on the edge of the moor that surrounds the sunken village of Aven-a-Christ. Madame Lavigne, who was knitting stockings—for she lived by knitting stockings—heard, as she thought, a passing of feet, and what seemed like a tap at the door. She dismissed the idea, for who would be passing at such an hour, and where there was no road? But a few minutes later the tapping came again, and Madame Lavigne, taking her candle in her hand, went to see who was there. The instant she released the latch a gust of wind blew out the candle, and Madame Lavigne could see no one. She called, but there was no answer. She was about to close the door again when she heard a faint sound. It was not exactly a cry. It was as if someone she could not see, in the tiniest of voices, had said something she could not understand.

Madame Lavigne crossed herself and muttered a prayer, and then she heard it again. It seemed to come from close at her feet, and feeling with her hands—for she thought it might be a stray cat—she found quite a large parcel, It was warm and soft, though, of course, a bit wet, and Madame Lavigne brought it in, and having closed the door and re-lit her candle, laid it on the table. And then she saw it was the tiniest of babies.

It must always be a difficult situation. Madame Lavigne did what most people would have done in the case. She unrolled the wrappings, and taking the little thing on her lap, sat down in front of the dull peat fire and considered. It seemed wonderfully contented, and Madame Lavigne thought the best thing to do would be to undress it and put it to bed, and then go on with her knitting. She would consult Father Jean in the morning and take his advice. She had never seen such fine clothes. She took them off one by one, lovingly feeling their texture, and when she finally removed the last little shift and the little white thing lay exposed, Madame Lavigne sprang up with a cry and all but dropped it into the fire. For she saw by the mark that every Breton peasant knows that it was not a child but a fairy.

Her proper course, as she well knew, was to have opened the door and flung it out into the darkness. Most women of the village would have done so, and spent the rest of the night on their knees. But some-one must have chosen with foresight. There came to Madame Lavigne the memory of her good man and her three tall sons, taken from her one by one by the jealous sea, and, come what might of it, she could not do it. The little thing understood, that was clear, for it smiled quite knowingly and stretched out its little hands, touching Madame Lavigne's brown withered skin, and stirring forgotten beatings of her heart.

Father Jean—one takes him to have been a tolerant, gently wise old gentleman—could see no harm. That is, if Madame Lavigne could afford the luxury. Maybe it was a good fairy. Would bring her luck. And certain it is that the cackling of Madame's hens was heard more often than before, and the weeds seemed fewer in the little patch of garden that Madame Lavigne had rescued from the moor.

Of course, the news spread. One gathers that Madame Lavigne rather gave herself airs. But the neighbours shook their heads, and the child grew up lonely and avoided. Fortunately, the cottage was far from other houses, and there was always the great moor with its deep hiding-places. Father Jean was her sole playmate. He would take her with him on his long tramps through his scattered district, leaving her screened among the furze and bracken near to the solitary farmsteads where he made his visitations.

He had learnt it was useless: all attempt of Mother Church to scold out of this sea and moor-girt flock their pagan superstitions. He would leave it to time. Later, perhaps opportunity might occur to place the child in some convent, where she would learn to forget, and grow into a good Catholic. Meanwhile, one had to take pity on the little lonely creature. Not entirely for her own sake maybe; a dear affectionate little soul strangely wise; so she seemed to Father Jean. Under the shade of trees or sharing warm shelter with the soft-eyed cows, he would teach her from his small stock of knowledge. Every now and then she would startle him with an intuition, a comment strangely unchildlike. It was as if she had known all about it, long ago. Father Jean would steal a swift glance at her from under his shaggy eyebrows and fall into a silence. It was curious also how the wild things of the field and wood seemed unafraid of her. At times, returning to where he had left her hidden, he would pause, wondering to whom she was talking, and then as he drew nearer would hear the stealing away of little feet, the startled flutter of wings. She had elfish ways, of which it seemed impossible to cure her. Often the good man, returning from some late visit of mercy with his lantern and his stout oak cudgel, would pause and listen to a wandering voice. It was never near enough for him to hear the words, and the voice was strange to him, though he knew it could be no one else. Madame Lavigne would shrug her shoulders. How could she help it? It was not for her to cross the "child," even sup-posing bolts and bars likely to be of any use. Father Jean gave it up in despair. Neither was it for him either to be too often forbidding and lecturing. Maybe the cunning tender ways had wove their web about the childless old gentleman's heart, making him also somewhat afraid. Perhaps other distractions! For Madame Lavigne would never allow her to do anything but the lightest of work. He would teach her to read. So quickly she learnt that it seemed to Father Jean she must be making believe not to have known it already. But he had his reward in watching the joy with which she would devour, for preference, the quaint printed volumes of romance and history that he would bring home to her from his rare journeyings to the distant town.

It was when she was about thirteen that the ladies and gentlemen came from Paris. Of course they were not real ladies and gentlemen. Only a little company of artists seeking new fields. They had "done" the coast and the timbered houses of the narrow streets, and one of them had suggested exploring the solitary, unknown inlands. They came across her seated on an old grey stone reading from an ancient-looking book, and she had risen and curtsied to them. She was never afraid. It was she who excited fear. Often she would look after the children flying from her, feeling a little sad. But, of course, it could not be helped. She was a fairy. She would have done them no harm, but this they could not be expected to understand. It was a delightful change; meeting human beings who neither screamed nor hastily recited their paternosters, but who, instead, returned one's smile. They asked her where she lived, and she showed them. They were staying at Aven-a-Christ; and one of the ladies was brave enough even to kiss her. Laughing and talking they all walked down the hill together. They found Madame Lavigne working in her garden. Madame Lavigne washed her hands of all responsibility. It was for Suzanne to decide. It seemed they wanted to make a picture of her, sitting on the grey stone where they had found her. It was surely only kind to let them; so next morning she was there again waiting for them. They gave her a five-franc piece. Madame Lavigne was doubtful of handling it, but Father Jean vouched for it as being good Republican money; and as the days went by Madame Lavigne's black stocking grew heavier and heavier as she hung it again each night in the chimney.

It was the lady who had first kissed her that discovered who she was. They had all of them felt sure from the beginning that she was a fairy, and that "Suzanne" could not be her real name. They found it in the "Heptameron of Friar Bonnet. In which is recorded the numerous adventures of the valiant and puissant King Ryence of Bretagne," which one of them had picked up on the Quai aux Fleurs and brought with him. It told all about the White Ladies, and therein she was described. There could be no mistaking her; the fair body that was like to a willow swayed by the wind. The white feet that could pass, leaving the dew unshaken from the grass. The eyes blue and deep as mountain lakes. The golden locks of which the sun was jealous.

It was all quite clear. She was Malvina, once favourite to Harbundia, Queen of the White Ladies of Brittany. For reasons—further allusion to which politeness forbade—she had been a wanderer, no one knowing what had become of her. And now the whim had taken her to reappear as a little Breton peasant girl, near to the scene of her past glories. They knelt before her, offering her homage, and all the ladies kissed her. The gentlemen of the party thought their turn would follow. But it never did. It was not their own shyness that stood in their way: one must do them that justice. It was as if some youthful queen, exiled and unknown amongst strangers, had been suddenly recognised by a little band of her faithful subjects, passing by chance that way. So that, instead of frolic and laughter, as had been intended, they remained standing with bared heads; and no one liked to be the first to speak.

She put them at their ease—or tried to—with a gracious gesture. But enjoined upon them all her wish for secrecy. And so dismissed they seem to have returned to the village a marvellously sober little party, experiencing all the sensations of honest folk admitted to their first glimpse of high society.

They came again next year—at least a few of them—bringing with them a dress more worthy of Malvina's wearing. It was as near as Paris could achieve to the true and original costume as described by the good Friar Bonnet, the which had been woven in a single night by the wizard spider Karai out of moonlight. Malvina accepted it with gracious thanks, and was evidently pleased to find herself again in fit and proper clothes. It was hidden away for rare occasions where only Malvina knew. But the lady who had first kissed her, and whose speciality was fairies, craving permission, Malvina consented to wear it while sitting for her portrait. The picture one may still see in the Palais des Beaux Arts at Nantes (the Bretonne Room). It represents her standing straight as an arrow, a lone little figure in the centre of a treeless moor. The painting of the robe is said to be very wonderful. "Malvina of Brittany" is the inscription, the date being Nineteen Hundred and Thirteen.

The next year Malvina was no longer there. Madame Lavigne, folding knotted hands, had muttered her last paternoster. Pere Jean had urged the convent. But for the first time, with him, she had been frankly obstinate. Some fancy seemed to have got into the child's head. Something that she evidently connected with the vast treeless moor rising southward to where the ancient menhir of King Taramis crowned its summit. The good man yielded, as usual. For the present there were Madame Lavigne's small savings. Suzanne's wants were but few. The rare shopping necessary Father Jean could see to himself. With the coming of winter he would broach the subject again, and then be quite firm. Just these were the summer nights when Suzanne loved to roam; and as for danger! there was not a lad for ten leagues round who would not have run a mile to avoid passing, even in daylight, that cottage standing where the moor dips down to the sealands.

But one surmises that even a fairy may feel lonesome. Especially a banished fairy, hanging as it were between earth and air, knowing mortal maidens kissed and courted, while one's own companions kept away from one in hiding. Maybe the fancy came to her that, after all these years, they might forgive her. Still, it was their meeting place, so legend ran, especially of midsummer nights. Rare it was now for human eye to catch a glimpse of the shimmering robes, but high on the tree-less moor to the music of the Lady of the Fountain, one might still hear, were one brave enough to venture, the rhythm of their dancing feet. If she sought them, softly calling, might they not reveal themselves to her, make room for her once again in the whirling circle? One has the idea that the moonlight frock may have added to her hopes. Philosophy admits that feeling oneself well dressed gives confidence.

If all of them had not disappeared—been kissed three times upon the lips by mortal man and so become a woman? It seems to have been a possibility for which your White Lady had to be prepared. That is, if she chose to suffer it. If not, it was unfortunate for the too daring mortal. But if he gained favour in her eyes! That he was brave, his wooing proved. If, added thereto, he were comely, with kind strong ways, and eyes that drew you? History proves that such dreams must have come even to White Ladies. Maybe more especially on midsummer nights when the moon is at its full. It was on such a night that Sir Gerylon had woke Malvina's sister Sighile with a kiss. A true White Lady must always dare to face her fate.

It seems to have befallen Malvina. Some told Father Jean how he had arrived in a chariot drawn by winged horses, the thunder of his passing waking many in the sleeping villages beneath. And others how he had come in the form of a great bird. Father Jean had heard strange sounds himself, and certain it was that Suzanne had disappeared.

Father Jean heard another version a few weeks later, told him by an English officer of Engineers who had ridden from the nearest station on a bicycle and who arrived hot and ravenously thirsty. And Father Jean, under promise of seeing Suzanne on the first opportunity, believed it. But to most of his flock it sounded an impossible rigmarole, told for the purpose of disguising the truth.

So ends my story—or rather the story I have pieced together from information of a contradictory nature received. Whatever you make of it; whether with the Doctor you explain it away; or whether with Professor Littlecherry, LL.D., F.R.S., you believe the world not altogether explored and mapped, the fact remains that Malvina of Brittany has passed away. To the younger Mrs. Raffleton, listening on the Sussex Downs to dull, distant sounds that make her heart beat, and very nervous of telegraph boys, has come already some of the disadvantages attendant on her new rank of womanhood. And yet one gathers, looking down into those strange deep eyes, that she would not change anything about her, even if now she could.

THE STREET OF THE BLANK WALL

I had turned off from the Edgware Road into a street leading west, the atmosphere of which had appealed to me. It was a place of quiet houses standing behind little gardens. They had the usual names printed on the stuccoed gateposts. The fading twilight was just sufficient to enable one to read them. There was a Laburnum Villa, and The Cedars, and a Cairngorm, rising to the height of three storeys, with a curious little turret that branched out at the top, and was crowned with a conical roof, so that it looked as if wearing a witch's hat. Especially when two small windows just below the eaves sprang suddenly into light, and gave one the feeling of a pair of wicked eyes suddenly flashed upon one.

The street curved to the right, ending in an open space through which passed a canal beneath a low arched bridge. There were still the same quiet houses behind their small gardens, and I watched for a while the lamplighter picking out the shape of the canal, that widened just above the bridge into a lake with an island in the middle. After that I must have wandered in a circle, for later on I found myself back in the same spot, though I do not suppose I had passed a dozen people on my way; and then I set to work to find my way back to Paddington.

I thought I had taken the road by which I had come, but the half light must have deceived me. Not that it mattered. They had a lurking mystery about them, these silent streets with their suggestion of hushed movement behind drawn curtains, of whispered voices behind the flimsy walls. Occasionally there would escape the sound of laughter, suddenly stifled as it seemed, and once the sudden cry of a child.

It was in a short street of semi-detached villas facing a high blank wall that, as I passed, I saw a blind move half-way up, revealing a woman's face. A gas lamp, the only one the street possessed, was nearly opposite. I thought at first it was the face of a girl, and then, as I looked again, it might have been the face of an old woman. One could not distinguish the colouring. In any case, the cold, blue gaslight would have made it seem pallid.

The remarkable feature was the eyes. It might have been, of course, that they alone caught the light and held it, rendering them uncannily large and brilliant. Or it might have been that the rest of the face was small and delicate, out of all proportion to them. She may have seen me, for the blind was drawn down again, and I passed on.

There was no particular reason why, but the incident lingered with me. The sudden raising of the blind, as of the curtain of some small theatre, the barely furnished room coming dimly into view, and the woman standing there, close to the footlights, as to my fancy it seemed. And then the sudden ringing down of the curtain before the play had begun. I turned at the corner of the street. The blind had been drawn up again, and I saw again the slight, girlish figure silhouetted against the side panes of the bow window.

At the same moment a man knocked up against me. It was not his fault. I had stopped abruptly, not giving him time to avoid me. We both apologised, blaming the darkness. It may have been my fancy, but I had the feeling that, instead of going on his way, he had turned and was following me. I waited till the next corner, and then swung round on my heel. But there was no sign of him, and after a while I found myself back in the Edgware Road.

Once or twice, in idle mood, I sought the street again, but without success; and the thing would, I expect, have faded from my memory, but that one evening, on my way home from Paddington, I came across the woman in the Harrow Road. There was no mistaking her. She almost touched me as she came out of a fishmonger's shop, and unconsciously, at the beginning, I found myself following her. This time I noticed the turnings, and five minutes' walking brought us to the street. Half a dozen times I must have been within a hundred yards of it. I lingered at the corner. She had not noticed me, and just as she reached the house a man came out of the shadows beyond the lamp-post and joined her.

I was due at a bachelor gathering that evening, and after dinner, the affair being fresh in my mind, I talked about it. I am not sure, but I think it was in connection with a discussion on Maeterlinck. It was that sudden lifting of the blind that had caught hold of me. As if, blundering into an empty theatre, I had caught a glimpse of some drama being played in secret. We passed to other topics, and when I was leaving a fellow guest asked me which way I was going. I told him, and, it being a fine night, he proposed that we should walk together. And in the quiet of Harley Street he confessed that his desire had not been entirely the pleasure of my company.

"It is rather curious," he said, "but today there suddenly came to my remembrance a case that for nearly eleven years I have never given a thought to. And now, on top of it, comes your description of that woman's face. I am wondering if it can be the same."

"It was the eyes," I said, "that struck me as so remarkable."

"It was the eyes that I chiefly remember her by," he replied. "Would you know the street again?"

We walked a little while in silence.

"It may seem, perhaps, odd to you," I answered, "but it would trouble me, the idea of any harm coming to her through me. What was the case?"

"You can feel quite safe on that point," he assured me. "I was her counsel—that is, if it is the same woman. How was she dressed?"

I could not see the reason for his question. He could hardly expect her to be wearing the clothes of eleven years ago.

"I don't think I noticed," I answered. "Some sort of a blouse, I suppose." And then I recollected. "Ah, yes, there was something uncommon," I added. "An unusually broad band of velvet, it looked like, round her neck."

"I thought so," he said. "Yes. It must be the same."

We had reached Marylebone Road, where our ways parted.

"I will look you up to-morrow afternoon, if I may," he said. "We might take a stroll round together."

He called on me about half-past five, and we reached the street just as the one solitary gas-lamp had been lighted. I pointed out the house to him, and he crossed over and looked at the number.

"Quite right," he said, on returning. "I made inquiries this morning. She was released six weeks ago on ticket-of-leave."

He took my arm.

"Not much use hanging about," he said. "The blind won't go up to-night. Rather a clever idea, selecting a house just opposite a lamp-post."

He had an engagement that evening; but later on he told me the story—that is, so far as he then knew it.

It was in the early days of the garden suburb movement. One of the first sites chosen was off the Finchley Road. The place was in the building, and one of the streets—Laleham Gardens—had only some half a dozen houses in it, all unoccupied save one. It was a lonely, loose end of the suburb, terminating suddenly in open fields. From the unfinished end of the road the ground sloped down somewhat steeply to a pond, and beyond that began a small wood. The one house occupied had been bought by a young married couple named Hepworth.

The husband was a good-looking, pleasant young fellow. Being clean-shaven, his exact age was difficult to judge. The wife, it was quite evident, was little more than a girl. About the man there was a suggestion of weakness. At least, that was the impression left on the mind of the house-agent. To-day he would decide, and to-morrow he changed his mind. Jetson, the agent, had almost given up hope of bringing off a deal. In the end it was Mrs. Hepworth who, taking the matter into her own hands, fixed upon the house in Laleham Gardens. Young Hepworth found fault with it on the ground of its isolation. He himself was often away for days at a time, travelling on business, and was afraid she would be nervous. He had been very persistent on this point; but in whispered conversations she had persuaded him out of his objection. It was one of those pretty, fussy little houses; and it seemed to have taken her fancy. Added to which, according to her argument, it was just within their means, which none of the others were. Young Hepworth may have given the usual references, but if so they were never taken up. The house was sold on the company's usual terms. The deposit was paid by a cheque, which was duly cleared, and the house itself was security for the rest. The company's solicitor, with Hepworth's consent, acted for both parties.

It was early in June when the Hepworths moved in. They furnished only one bedroom; and kept no servant, a charwoman coming in every morning and going away about six in the evening. Jetson was their nearest neighbour. His wife and daughters called on them, and confess to have taken a liking to them both. Indeed, between one of the Jetson girls, the youngest, and Mrs. Hepworth there seems to have sprung up a close friendship. Young Hepworth, the husband, was always charming, and evidently took great pains to make himself agreeable. But with regard to him they had the feeling that he was never altogether at his ease. They described him—though that, of course, was after the event—as having left upon them the impression of a haunted man.

There was one occasion in particular. It was about ten o'clock. The Jetsons had been spending the evening with the Hepworths, and were just on the point of leaving, when there came a sudden, clear knock at the door. It turned out to be Jetson's foreman, who had to leave by an early train in the morning, and had found that he needed some further instructions. But the terror in Hepworth's face was unmistakable. He had turned a look towards his wife that was almost of despair; and it had seemed to the Jetsons—or, talking it over afterwards, they may have suggested the idea to each other—that there came a flash of contempt into her eyes, though it yielded the next instant to an expression of pity. She had risen, and already moved some steps towards the door, when young Hepworth had stopped her, and gone out himself. But the curious thing was that, according to the foreman's account, Hepworth never opened the front door, but came upon him stealthily from behind. He must have slipped out by the back and crept round the house.

The incident had puzzled the Jetsons, especially that involuntary flash of contempt that had come into Mrs. Hepworth's eyes. She had always appeared to adore her husband, and of the two, if possible, to be the one most in love with the other. They had no friends or acquaintances except the Jetsons. No one else among their neighbours had taken the trouble to call on them, and no stranger to the suburb had, so far as was known, ever been seen in Laleham Gardens.

Until one evening a little before Christmas.

Jetson was on his way home from his office in the Finchley Road. There had been a mist hanging about all day, and with nightfall it had settled down into a whitish fog. Soon after leaving the Finchley Road, Jetson noticed in front of him a man wearing a long, yellow mackintosh, and some sort of soft felt hat. He gave Jetson the idea of being a sailor; it may have been merely the stiff, serviceable mackintosh. At the corner of Laleham Gardens the man turned, and glanced up at the name upon the lamp-post, so that Jetson had a full view of him. Evidently it was the street for which he was looking. Jetson, somewhat curious, the Hepworths' house being still the only one occupied, paused at the corner, and watched. The Hepworths' house was, of course, the only one in the road that showed any light. The man, when he came to the gate, struck a match for the purpose of reading the number. Satisfied it was the house he wanted, he pushed open the gate and went up the path.

But, instead of using the bell or knocker, Jetson was surprised to hear him give three raps on the door with his stick. There was no answer, and Jetson, whose interest was now thoroughly aroused, crossed to the other corner, from where he could command a better view. Twice the man repeated his three raps on the door, each time a little louder, and the third time the door was opened. Jetson could not tell by whom, for whoever it was kept behind it.

He could just see one wall of the passage, with a pair of old naval cutlasses crossed above the picture of a three-masted schooner that he knew hung there. The door was opened just sufficient, and the man slipped in, and the door was closed behind him. Jetson had turned to continue his way, when the fancy seized him to give one glance back. The house was in complete darkness, though a moment before Jetson was positive there had been a light in the ground floor window.

It all sounded very important afterwards, but at the time there was nothing to suggest to Jetson anything very much out of the common. Because for six months no friend or relation had called to see them, that was no reason why one never should. In the fog, a stranger may have thought it simpler to knock at the door with his stick than to fumble in search of a bell. The Hepworths lived chiefly in the room at the back. The light in the drawing-room may have been switched off for economy's sake. Jetson recounted the incident on reaching home, not as anything remarkable, but just as one mentions an item of gossip. The only one who appears to have attached any meaning to the affair was Jetson's youngest daughter, then a girl of eighteen. She asked one or two questions about the man, and, during the evening, slipped out by herself and ran round to the Hepworths. She found the house empty. At all events, she could obtain no answer, and the place, back and front, seemed to her to be uncannily silent.

Jetson called the next morning, something of his daughter's un-easiness having communicated itself to him. Mrs. Hepworth herself opened the door to him. In his evidence at the trial, Jetson admitted that her appearance had startled him. She seems to have anticipated his questions by at once explaining that she had had news of an un-pleasant nature, and had been worrying over it all night. Her husband had been called away suddenly to America, where it would be neces-sary for her to join him as soon as possible. She would come round to Jetson's office later in the day to make arrangements about getting rid of the house and furniture.

The story seemed to reasonably account for the stranger's visit, and Jetson, expressing his sympathy and promising all help in his power, continued his way to the office. She called in the afternoon and handed him over the keys, retaining one for herself. She wished the furniture to be sold by auction, and he was to accept almost any offer for the house. She would try and see him again before sailing; if not, she would write him with her address. She was perfectly cool and collected. She had called on his wife and daughters in the afternoon, and had wished them good-bye.

Outside Jetson's office she hailed a cab, and returned in it to Laleham Gardens to collect her boxes. The next time Jetson saw her she was in the dock, charged with being an accomplice in the murder of her husband.

The body had been discovered in a pond some hundred yards from the unfinished end of Laleham Gardens. A house was in course of erection on a neighbouring plot, and a workman, in dipping up a pail of water, had dropped in his watch. He and his mate, worrying round with a rake, had drawn up pieces of torn clothing, and this, of course, had led to the pond being properly dragged. Otherwise the discovery might never have been made.

The body, heavily weighted with a number of flat-irons fastened to it by a chain and padlock, had sunk deep into the soft mud, and might have remained there till it rotted. A valuable gold repeater, that Jetson remembered young Hepworth having told him had been a presentation to his father, was in its usual pocket, and a cameo ring that Hepworth had always worn on his third finger was likewise fished up from the mud. Evidently the murder belonged to the category of crimes passionel. The theory of the prosecution was that it had been committed by a man who, before her marriage, had been Mrs. Hepworth's lover.

The evidence, contrasted with the almost spiritually beautiful face of the woman in the dock, came as a surprise to everyone in court. Originally connected with an English circus troupe touring in Holland, she appears, about seventeen, to have been engaged as a "song and dance artiste" at a particularly shady cafe chantant in Rotterdam, frequented chiefly by sailors. From there a man, an English sailor known as Charlie Martin, took her away, and for some months she had lived with him at a small estaminet the other side of the river. Later, they left Rotterdam and came to London, where they took lodgings in Poplar, near to the docks.

It was from this address in Poplar that, some ten months before the murder, she had married young Hepworth. What had become of Martin was not known. The natural assumption was that, his money being exhausted, he had returned to his calling, though his name, for some reason, could not be found in any ship's list.

That he was one and the same with the man that Jetson had watched till the door of the Hepworths' house had closed upon him there could be no doubt. Jetson described him as a thick-set, handsome-looking man, with a reddish beard and moustache. Earlier in the day he had been seen at Hampstead, where he had dined at a small coffee-shop in the High Street. The girl who had waited on him had also been struck by the bold, piercing eyes and the curly red beard. It had been an off-time, between two and three, when he had dined there, and the girl admitted that she had found him a "pleasant-spoken gentleman," and "inclined to be merry." He had told her that he had arrived in England only three days ago, and that he hoped that evening to see his sweetheart. He had accompanied the words with a laugh, and the girl thought—though, of course, this may have been after-suggestion—that an ugly look followed the laugh.

One imagines that it was this man's return that had been the fear constantly haunting young Hepworth. The three raps on the door, it was urged by the prosecution, was a pre-arranged or pre-understood signal, and the door had been opened by the woman. Whether the husband was in the house, or whether they waited for him, could not be said. He been killed by a bullet entering through the back of the neck; the man had evidently come prepared.

Ten days had elapsed between the murder and the finding of the body, and the man was never traced. A postman had met him coming from the neighbourhood of Laleham Gardens at about half-past nine. In the fog, they had all but bumped into one another, and the man had immediately turned away his face.

About the soft felt hat there was nothing to excite attention, but the long, stiff, yellow mackintosh was quite unusual. The postman had caught only a momentary glimpse of the face, but was certain it was clean shaven. This made a sensation in court for the moment, but only until the calling of the next witness. The charwoman usually employed by the Hepworths had not been admitted to the house on the morning of Mrs. Hepworth's departure. Mrs. Hepworth had met her at the door and paid her a week's money in lieu of notice, explaining to her that she would not be wanted any more. Jetson, thinking he might possibly do better by letting the house furnished, had sent for this woman, and instructed her to give the place a thorough cleaning. Sweeping the carpet in the dining-room with a dustpan and brush, she had discovered a number of short red hairs. The man, before leaving the house, had shaved himself.

That he had still retained the long, yellow mackintosh may have been with the idea of starting a false clue. Having served its purpose, it could be discarded. The beard would not have been so easy. What roundabout way he may have taken one cannot say, but it must have been some time during the night or early morning that he reached young Hepworth's office in Fenchurch Street. Mrs. Hepworth had evidently provided him with the key.

There he seems to have hidden the hat and mackintosh and to have taken in exchange some clothes belonging to the murdered man. Hepworth's clerk, Ellenby, an elderly man—of the type that one generally describes as of gentlemanly appearance—was accustomed to his master being away unexpectedly on business, which was that of a ships' furnisher. He always kept an overcoat and a bag ready packed in the office. Missing them, Ellenby had assumed that his master had been called away by an early train. He would have been worried after a few days, but that he had received a telegram—as he then supposed from his master—explaining that young Hepworth had gone to Ireland and would be away for some days. It was nothing unusual for Hepworth to be absent, superintending the furnishing of a ship, for a fortnight at a time, and nothing had transpired in the office necessitating special instructions. The telegram had been handed in at Charing Cross, but the time chosen had been a busy period of the day, and no one had any recollection of the sender. Hepworth's clerk unhesitatingly identified the body as that of his employer, for whom it was evident that he had entertained a feeling of affection. About Mrs. Hepworth he said as little as he could. While she was awaiting her trial it had been necessary for him to see her once or twice with reference to the business. Previous to this, he knew nothing about her.

The woman's own attitude throughout the trial had been quite unexplainable. Beyond agreeing to a formal plea of "Not guilty," she had made no attempt to defend herself. What little assistance her solicitors had obtained had been given them, not by the woman herself, but by Hepworth's clerk, more for the sake of his dead master than out of any sympathy towards the wife. She herself appeared utterly indifferent. Only once had she been betrayed into a momentary emotion. It was when her solicitors were urging her almost angrily to give them some particulars upon a point they thought might be helpful to her case.

"He's dead!" she had cried out almost with a note of exultation. "Dead! Dead! What else matters?"

The next moment she had apologised for her outburst.

"Nothing can do any good," she had said. "Let the thing take its course."

It was the astounding callousness of the woman that told against her both with the judge and the jury. That shaving in the dining-room, the murdered man's body not yet cold! It must have been done with Hepworth's safety-razor. She must have brought it down to him, found him a looking-glass, brought him soap and water and a towel, afterwards removing all traces. Except those few red hairs that had clung, unnoticed, to the carpet. That nest of flat-irons used to weight the body! It must have been she who had thought of them. The idea would never have occurred to a man. The chain and padlock with which to fasten them. She only could have known that such things were in the house. It must have been she who had planned the exchange of clothes in Hepworth's office, giving him the key. She it must have been who had thought of the pond, holding open the door while the man had staggered out under his ghastly burden; waited, keeping watch, listening to hear the splash.

Evidently it had been her intention to go off with the murderer—to live with him! That story about America. If all had gone well, it would have accounted for everything. After leaving Laleham Gardens she had taken lodgings in a small house in Kentish Town under the name of Howard, giving herself out to be a chorus singer, her husband being an actor on tour. To make the thing plausible, she had obtained employment in one of the pantomimes. Not for a moment had she lost her head. No one had ever called at her lodgings, and there had come no letters for her. Every hour of her day could be accounted for. Their plans must have been worked out over the corpse of her murdered husband. She was found guilty of being an "accessory after the fact," and sentenced to fifteen years' penal servitude.

That brought the story up to eleven years ago. After the trial, interested in spite of himself, my friend had ferreted out some further particulars. Inquiries at Liverpool had procured him the information that Hepworth's father, a shipowner in a small way, had been well known and highly respected. He was retired from business when he died, some three years previous to the date of the murder. His wife had survived him by only a few months. Besides Michael, the murdered son, there were two other children—an elder brother, who was thought to have gone abroad to one of the colonies, and a sister who had married a French naval officer. Either they had not heard of the case or had not wished to have their names dragged into it. Young Michael had started life as an architect, and was supposed to have been doing well, but after the death of his parents had disappeared from the neighbourhood, and, until the trial, none of his acquaintances up North ever knew what had become of him.

But a further item of knowledge that my friend's inquiries had elicited had somewhat puzzled him. Hepworth's clerk, Ellenby, had been the confidential clerk of Hepworth's father! He had entered the service of the firm as a boy; and when Hepworth senior retired, Ellenby—with the old gentleman's assistance—had started in business for himself as a ships' furnisher! Nothing of all this came out at the trial. Ellenby had not been cross-examined. There was no need for it. But it seemed odd, under all the circumstances, that he had not volunteered the information. It may, of course, have been for the sake of the brother and sister. Hepworth is a common enough name in the North. He may have hoped to keep the family out of connection with the case.

As regards the woman, my friend could learn nothing further beyond the fact that, in her contract with the music-hall agent in Rotterdam, she had described herself as the daughter of an English musician, and had stated that both her parents were dead. She may have engaged herself without knowing the character of the hall, and the man, Charlie Martin, with his handsome face and pleasing sailor ways, and at least an Englishman, may have seemed to her a welcome escape.

She may have been passionately fond of him, and young Hepworth—crazy about her, for she was beautiful enough to turn any man's head—may in Martin's absence have lied to her, told her he was dead—lord knows what!—to induce her to marry him. The murder may have seemed to her a sort of grim justice.

But even so, her cold-blooded callousness was surely abnormal! She had married him, lived with him for nearly a year. To the Jetsons she had given the impression of being a woman deeply in love with her husband. It could not have been mere acting kept up day after day.

"There was something else." We were discussing the case in my friend's chambers. His brief of eleven years ago was open before him. He was pacing up and down with his hands in his pockets, thinking as he talked. "Something that never came out. There was a curious feeling she gave me in that moment when sentence was pronounced upon her. It was as if, instead of being condemned, she had triumphed. Acting! If she had acted during the trial, pretended remorse, even pity, I could have got her off with five years. She seemed to be unable to disguise the absolute physical relief she felt at the thought that he was dead, that his hand would never again touch her. There must have been something that had suddenly been revealed to her, something that had turned her love to hate.

"There must be something fine about the man, too." That was another suggestion that came to him as he stood staring out of the window across the river. "She's paid and has got her receipt, but he is still 'wanted.' He is risking his neck every evening he watches for the raising of that blind."

His thought took another turn.

"Yet how could he have let her go through those ten years of living death while he walked the streets scot free? Some time during the trial—the evidence piling up against her day by day—why didn't he come forward, if only to stand beside her? Get himself hanged, if only out of mere decency?"

He sat down, took the brief up in his hand without looking at it.

"Or was that the reward that she claimed? That he should wait, keeping alive the one hope that would make the suffering possible to her? Yes," he continued, musing, "I can see a man who cared for a woman taking that as his punishment."

Now that his interest in the case had been revived he seemed unable to keep it out of his mind. Since our joint visit I had once or twice passed through the street by myself, and on the last occasion had again seen the raising of the blind. It obsessed him—the desire to meet the man face to face. A handsome, bold, masterful man, he conceived him. But there must be something more for such a woman to have sold her soul—almost, one might say—for the sake of him.

There was just one chance of succeeding. Each time he had come from the direction of the Edgware Road. By keeping well out of sight at the other end of the street, and watching till he entered it, one might time oneself to come upon him just under the lamp. He would hardly be likely to turn and go back; that would be to give himself away. He would probably content himself with pretending to be like ourselves, merely hurrying through, and in his turn watching till we had disappeared.

Fortune seemed inclined to favour us. About the usual time the blind was gently raised, and very soon afterwards there came round the corner the figure of a man. We entered the street ourselves a few seconds later, and it seemed likely that, as we had planned, we should come face to face with him under the gaslight. He walked towards us, stooping and with bent head. We expected him to pass the house by. To our surprise he stopped when he came to it, and pushed open the gate. In another moment we should have lost all chance of seeing anything more of him except his bent back. With a couple of strides my friend was behind him. He laid his hand on the man's shoulder and forced him to turn round. It was an old, wrinkled face with gentle, rather watery eyes.

We were both so taken aback that for a moment we could say nothing. My friend stammered out an apology about having mistaken the house, and rejoined me. At the corner we burst out laughing almost simultaneously. And then my friend suddenly stopped and stared at me.

"Hepworth's old clerk!" he said. "Ellenby!"

It seemed to him monstrous. The man had been more than a clerk. The family had treated him as a friend. Hepworth's father had set him up in business. For the murdered lad he had had a sincere attachment; he had left that conviction on all of them. What was the meaning of it?

A directory was on the mantelpiece. It was the next afternoon. I had called upon him in his chambers. It was just an idea that came to me. I crossed over and opened it, and there was his name, "Ellenby and Co., Ships' Furnishers," in a court off the Minories.

Was he helping her for the sake of his dead master—trying to get her away from the man. But why? The woman had stood by and watched the lad murdered. How could he bear even to look on her again?

Unless there had been that something that had not come out—something he had learnt later—that excused even that monstrous callousness of hers.

Yet what could there be? It had all been so planned, so cold-blooded. That shaving in the dining-room! It was that seemed most to stick in his throat. She must have brought him down a looking-glass; there was not one in the room. Why couldn't he have gone upstairs into the bathroom, where Hepworth always shaved himself, where he would have found everything to his hand?

He had been moving about the room, talking disjointedly as he paced, and suddenly he stopped and looked at me.

"Why in the dining-room?" he demanded of me.

He was jingling some keys in his pocket. It was a habit of his when cross-examining, and I felt as if somehow I knew; and, without thinking—so it seemed to me—I answered him.

"Perhaps," I said, "it was easier to bring a razor down than to carry a dead man up."

He leant with his arms across the table, his eyes glittering with excitement.

"Can't you see it?" he said. "That little back parlour with its fussy ornaments. The three of them standing round the table, Hepworth's hands nervously clutching a chair. The reproaches, the taunts, the threats. Young Hepworth—he struck everyone as a weak man, a man physically afraid—white, stammering, not knowing which way to look. The woman's eyes turning from one to the other. That flash of contempt again—she could not help it—followed, worse still, by pity. If only he could have answered back, held his own! If only he had not been afraid! And then that fatal turning away with a sneering laugh one imagines, the bold, dominating eyes no longer there to cower him.

"That must have been the moment. The bullet, if you remember, entered through the back of the man's neck. Hepworth must always have been picturing to himself this meeting—tenants of garden suburbs do not carry loaded revolvers as a habit—dwelling upon it till he had worked himself up into a frenzy of hate and fear. Weak men always fly to extremes. If there was no other way, he would kill him.

"Can't you hear the silence? After the reverberations had died away! And then they are both down on their knees, patting him, feeling for his heart. The man must have gone down like a felled ox; there were no traces of blood on the carpet. The house is far from any neighbour; the shot in all probability has not been heard. If only they can get rid of the body! The pond—not a hundred yards away!"

He reached for the brief, still lying among his papers; hurriedly turned the scored pages.

"What easier? A house being built on the very next plot. Wheelbarrows to be had for the taking. A line of planks reaching down to the edge. Depth of water where the body was discovered four feet six inches. Nothing to do but just tip up the barrow.

"Think a minute. Must weigh him down, lest he rise to accuse us; weight him heavily, so that he will sink lower and lower into the soft mud, lie there till he rots.

"Think again. Think it out to the end. Suppose, in spite of all our precautions, he does rise? Suppose the chain slips? The workmen going to and fro for water—suppose they do discover him?

"He is lying on his back, remember. They would have turned him over to feel for his heart. Have closed his eyes, most probably, not liking their stare.

"It would be the woman who first thought of it. She has seen them both lying with closed eyes beside her. It may have always been in her mind, the likeness between them. With Hepworth's watch in his pocket, Hepworth's ring on his finger! If only it was not for the beard—that fierce, curling, red beard!

"They creep to the window and peer out. Fog still thick as soup. Not a soul, not a sound. Plenty of time.

"Then to get away, to hide till one is sure. Put on the mackintosh. A man in a yellow mackintosh may have been seen to enter; let him be seen to go away. In some dark corner or some empty railway carriage take it off and roll it up. Then make for the office. Wait there for Ellenby. True as steel, Ellenby; good business man. Be guided by Ellenby."

He flung the brief from him with a laugh.

"Why, there's not a missing link!" he cried. "And to think that not a fool among us ever thought of it!"

"Everything fitting into its place," I suggested, "except young Hepworth. Can you see him, from your description of him, sitting down and coolly elaborating plans for escape, the corpse of the murdered man stretched beside him on the hearthrug?"

"No," he answered. "But I can see her doing it, a woman who for week after week kept silence while we raged and stormed at her, a woman who for three hours sat like a statue while old Cutbush painted her to a crowded court as a modern Jezebel, who rose up from her seat when that sentence of fifteen years' penal servitude was pronounced upon her with a look of triumph in her eyes, and walked out of court as if she had been a girl going to meet her lover.

"I'll wager," he added, "it was she who did the shaving. Hepworth would have cut him, even with a safety-razor."

"It must have been the other one, Martin," I said, "that she loathed. That almost exultation at the thought that he was dead," I reminded him.

"Yes," he mused. "She made no attempt to disguise it. Curious there having been that likeness between them." He looked at his watch. "Do you care to come with me?" he said.

"Where are you going?" I asked him.

"We may just catch him," he answered. "Ellenby and Co."

The office was on the top floor of an old-fashioned house in a cul-de-sac off the Minories. Mr. Ellenby was out, so the lanky office-boy informed us, but would be sure to return before evening; and we sat and waited by the meagre fire till, as the dusk was falling, we heard his footsteps on the creaking stairs.

He halted a moment in the doorway, recognising us apparently without surprise; and then, with a hope that we had not been kept waiting long, he led the way into an inner room.

"I do not suppose you remember me," said my friend, as soon as the door was closed. "I fancy that, until last night, you never saw me without my wig and gown. It makes a difference. I was Mrs. Hepworth's senior counsel."

It was unmistakable, the look of relief that came into the old, dim eyes. Evidently the incident of the previous evening had suggested to him an enemy.

"You were very good," he murmured. "Mrs. Hepworth was overwrought at the time, but she was very grateful, I know, for all your efforts."

I thought I detected a faint smile on my friend's lips.

"I must apologise for my rudeness to you of last night," he continued. "I expected, when I took the liberty of turning you round, that I was going to find myself face to face with a much younger man."

"I took you to be a detective," answered Ellenby, in his soft, gentle voice. "You will forgive me, I'm sure. I am rather short-sighted. Of course, I can only conjecture, but if you will take my word, I can assure you that Mrs. Hepworth has never seen or heard from the man Charlie Martin since the date of"—he hesitated a moment—"of the murder."

"It would have been difficult," agreed my friend, "seeing that Charlie Martin lies buried in Highgate Cemetery."

Old as he was, he sprang from his chair, white and trembling.

"What have you come here for?" he demanded.

"I took more than a professional interest in the case," answered my friend. "Ten years ago I was younger than I am now. It may have been her youth—her extreme beauty. I think Mrs. Hepworth, in allowing her husband to visit her—here where her address is known to the police, and watch at any moment may be set upon her—is placing him in a position of grave danger. If you care to lay before me any facts that will allow me to judge of the case, I am prepared to put my experience, and, if need be, my assistance, at her service."

His self-possession had returned to him.

"If you will excuse me," he said, "I will tell the boy that he can go."

We heard him, a moment later, turn the key in the outer door; and when he came back and had made up the fire, he told us the beginning of the story.

The name of the man buried in Highgate Cemetery was Hepworth, after all. Not Michael, but Alex, the elder brother.

From boyhood he had been violent, brutal, unscrupulous. Judging from Ellenby's story, it was difficult to accept him as a product of modern civilisation. Rather he would seem to have been a throwback to some savage, buccaneering ancestor. To expect him to work, while he could live in vicious idleness at somebody else's expense, was found to be hopeless. His debts were paid for about the third or fourth time, and he was shipped off to the Colonies. Unfortunately, there were no means of keeping him there. So soon as the money provided him had been squandered, he returned, demanding more by menaces and threats. Meeting with unexpected firmness, he seems to have regarded theft and forgery as the only alternative left to him. To save him from punishment and the family name from disgrace, his parents' savings were sacrificed. It was grief and shame that, according to Ellenby, killed them both within a few months of one another.

Deprived by this blow of what he no doubt had come to consider his natural means of support, and his sister, fortunately for herself, being well out of his reach, he next fixed upon his brother Michael as his stay-by. Michael, weak, timid, and not perhaps without some remains of boyish affection for a strong, handsome, elder brother, foolishly yielded. The demands, of course, increased, until, in the end, it came almost as a relief when the man's vicious life led to his getting mixed up with a crime of a particularly odious nature. He was anxious now for his own sake to get away, and Michael, with little enough to spare for himself, provided him with the means, on the solemn understanding that he would never return.

But the worry and misery of it all had left young Michael a broken man. Unable to concentrate his mind any longer upon his profession, his craving was to get away from all his old associations—to make a fresh start in life. It was Ellenby who suggested London and the ship furnishing business, where Michael's small remaining capital would be of service. The name of Hepworth would be valuable in shipping circles, and Ellenby, arguing this consideration, but chiefly with the hope of giving young Michael more interest in the business, had insisted that the firm should be Hepworth and Co.

They had not been started a year before the man returned, as usual demanding more money. Michael, acting under Ellenby's guidance, refused in terms that convinced his brother that the game of bullying was up. He waited a while, and then wrote pathetically that he was ill and starving. If only for the sake of his young wife, would not Michael come and see them?

This was the first they had heard of his marriage. There was just a faint hope that it might have effected a change, and Michael, against Ellenby's advice, decided to go. In a miserable lodging-house in the East End he found the young wife, but not his brother, who did not return till he was on the point of leaving. In the interval the girl seems to have confided her story to Michael.

She had been a singer, engaged at a music-hall in Rotterdam. There Alex Hepworth, calling himself Charlie Martin, had met her and made love to her. When he chose, he could be agreeable enough, and no doubt her youth and beauty had given to his protestations, for the time being, a genuine ring of admiration and desire. It was to escape from her surroundings, more than anything else, that she had consented. She was little more than a child, and anything seemed preferable to the nightly horror to which her life exposed her.

He had never married her. At least, that was her belief at the time. During his first drunken bout he had flung it in her face that the form they had gone through was mere bunkum. Unfortunately for her, this was a lie. He had always been coolly calculating. It was probably with the idea of a safe investment that he had seen to it that the ceremony had been strictly legal.

Her life with him, so soon as the first novelty of her had worn off, had been unspeakable. The band that she wore round her neck was to hide where, in a fit of savagery, because she had refused to earn money for him on the streets, he had tried to cut her throat. Now that she had got back to England she intended to leave him. If he followed and killed her she did not care.

It was for her sake that young Hepworth eventually offered to help his brother again, on the condition that he would go away by himself. To this the other agreed. He seems to have given a short display of remorse. There must have been a grin on his face as he turned away. His cunning eyes had foreseen what was likely to happen. The idea of blackmail was no doubt in his mind from the beginning. With the charge of bigamy as a weapon in his hand, he might rely for the rest of his life upon a steady and increasing income.

Michael saw his brother off as a second-class passenger on a ship bound for the Cape. Of course, there was little chance of his keeping his word, but there was always the chance of his getting himself knocked on the head in some brawl. Anyhow, he would be out of the way for a season, and the girl, Lola, would be left. A month later he married her, and four months after that received a letter from his brother containing messages to Mrs. Martin, "from her loving husband, Charlie," who hoped before long to have the pleasure of seeing her again.

Inquiries through the English Consul in Rotterdam proved that the threat was no mere bluff. The marriage had been legal and binding.

What happened on the night of the murder, was very much as my friend had reconstructed it. Ellenby, reaching the office at his usual time the next morning, had found Hepworth waiting for him. There he had remained in hiding until one morning, with dyed hair and a slight moustache, he had ventured forth.

Had the man's death been brought about by any other means, Ellenby would have counselled his coming forward and facing his trial, as he himself was anxious to do; but, viewed in conjunction with the relief the man's death must have been to both of them, that loaded revolver was too suggestive of premeditation. The isolation of the house, that conveniently near pond, would look as if thought of beforehand. Even if pleading extreme provocation, Michael escaped the rope, a long term of penal servitude would be inevitable.

Nor was it certain that even then the woman would go free. The murdered man would still, by a strange freak, be her husband; the murderer—in the eye of the law—her lover.

Her passionate will had prevailed. Young Hepworth had sailed for America. There he had no difficulty in obtaining employment—of course, under another name—in an architects office; and later had set up for himself. Since the night of the murder they had not seen each other till some three weeks ago.

I never saw the woman again. My friend, I believe, called on her. Hepworth had already returned to America, and my friend had succeeded in obtaining for her some sort of a police permit that practically left her free.

Sometimes of an evening I find myself passing through the street. And always I have the feeling of having blundered into an empty theatre—where the play is ended.

HIS EVENING OUT

The evidence of the park-keeper, David Bristow, of Gilder Street, Camden Town, is as follows:

I was on duty in St. James's Park on Thursday evening, my sphere extending from the Mall to the northern shore of the ornamental water east of the suspension bridge. At five-and-twenty to seven I took up a position between the peninsula and the bridge to await my colleague. He ought to have relieved me at half-past six, but did not arrive until a few minutes before seven, owing, so he explained, to the breaking down of his motor-'bus—which may have been true or may not, as the saying is.

I had just come to a halt, when my attention was arrested by a lady. I am unable to explain why the presence of a lady in St. James's Park should have seemed in any way worthy of notice except that, for certain reasons, she reminded me of my first wife. I observed that she hesitated between one of the public seats and two vacant chairs standing by themselves a little farther to the east. Eventually she selected one of the chairs, and, having cleaned it with an evening paper—the birds in this portion of the Park being extremely prolific—sat down upon it. There was plenty of room upon the public seat close to it, except for some children who were playing touch; and in consequence of this I judged her to be a person of means.

I walked to a point from where I could command the southern approaches to the bridge, my colleague arriving sometimes by way of Birdcage Walk and sometimes by way of the Horse Guards Parade. Not seeing any signs of him in the direction of the bridge, I turned back. A little way past the chair where the lady was sitting I met Mr.

Parable. I know Mr. Parable quite well by sight. He was wearing the usual grey suit and soft felt hat with which the pictures in the newspapers have made us all familiar. I judged that Mr. Parable had come from the Houses of Parliament, and the next morning my suspicions were confirmed by reading that he had been present at a tea-party given on the terrace by Mr. Will Crooks. Mr. Parable conveyed to me the suggestion of a man absorbed in thought, and not quite aware of what he was doing; but in this, of course, I may have been mistaken. He paused for a moment to look over the railings at the pelican. Mr. Parable said something to the pelican which I was not near enough to overhear; and then, still apparently in a state of abstraction, crossed the path and seated himself on the chair next to that occupied by the young lady.

From the tree against which I was standing I was able to watch the subsequent proceedings unobserved. The lady looked at Mr. Parable and then turned away and smiled to herself. It was a peculiar smile, and, again in some way I am unable to explain, reminded me of my first wife. It was not till the pelican put down his other leg and walked away that Mr. Parable, turning his gaze westward, became aware of the lady's presence.

From information that has subsequently come to my knowledge, I am prepared to believe that Mr. Parable, from the beginning, really thought the lady was a friend of his. What the lady thought is a matter for conjecture; I can only speak to the facts. Mr. Parable looked at the lady once or twice. Indeed, one might say with truth that he kept on doing it. The lady, it must be admitted, behaved for a while with extreme propriety; but after a time, as I felt must happen, their eyes met, and then it was I heard her say:

"Good evening, Mr. Parable."

She accompanied the words with the same peculiar smile to which I have already alluded. The exact words of Mr. Parable's reply I cannot remember. But it was to the effect that he had thought from the first that he had known her but had not been quite sure. It was at this point that, thinking I saw my colleague approaching, I went to meet him. I found I was mistaken, and slowly retraced my steps. I passed Mr. Parable and the lady. They were talking together with what I should describe as animation. I went as far as the southern extremity of the suspension bridge, and must have waited there quite ten minutes before returning eastward. It was while I was passing behind them on the grass, partially screened by the rhododendrons, that I heard Mr. Parable say to the lady:

"Why shouldn't we have it together?"

To which the lady replied:

"But what about Miss Clebb?"

I could not overhear what followed, owing to their sinking their voices. It seemed to be an argument. It ended with the young lady laughing and then rising. Mr. Parable also rose, and they walked off together. As they passed me I heard the lady say:

"I wonder if there's any place in London where you're not likely to be recognised."

Mr. Parable, who gave me the idea of being in a state of growing excitement, replied quite loudly:

"Oh, let 'em!"

I was following behind them when the lady suddenly stopped.

"I know!" she said. "The Popular Cafe."

The park-keeper said he was convinced he would know the lady again, having taken particular notice of her. She had brown eyes and was wearing a black hat supplemented with poppies.

Arthur Horton, waiter at the Popular Cafe, states as follows:

I know Mr. John Parable by sight. Have often heard him speak at public meetings. Am a bit of a Socialist myself. Remember his dining at the Popular Cafe on the evening of Thursday. Didn't recognise him immediately on his entrance for two reasons. One was his hat, and the other was his girl. I took it from him and hung it up. I mean, of course, the hat. It was a brand-new bowler, a trifle ikey about the brim. Have always associated him with a soft grey felt. But never with girls. Females, yes, to any extent. But this was the real article. You know what I mean—the sort of girl that you turn round to look after. It was she who selected the table in the corner behind the door. Been there before, I should say.

I should, in the ordinary course of business, have addressed Mr. Parable by name, such being our instructions in the case of customers known to us. But, putting the hat and the girl together, I decided not to. Mr. Parable was all for our three-and-six-penny table d'hote; he evidently not wanting to think. But the lady wouldn't hear of it.

"Remember Miss Clebb," she reminded him.

Of course, at the time I did not know what was meant. She ordered thin soup, a grilled sole, and cutlets au gratin. It certainly couldn't have been the dinner. With regard to the champagne, he would have his own way. I picked him out a dry '94, that you might have weaned a baby on. I suppose it was the whole thing combined.

It was after the sole that I heard Mr. Parable laugh. I could hardly credit my ears, but half-way through the cutlets he did it again.

There are two kinds of women. There is the woman who, the more she eats and drinks, the stodgier she gets, and the woman who lights up after it. I suggested a peche Melba between them, and when I returned with it, Mr. Parable was sitting with his elbows on the table gazing across at her with an expression that I can only describe as quite human. It was when I brought the coffee that he turned to me and asked:

"What's doing? Nothing stuffy," he added. "Is there an Exhibition anywhere—something in the open air?"

"You are forgetting Miss Clebb," the lady reminded him.

"For two pins," said Mr. Parable, "I would get up at the meeting and tell Miss Clebb what I really think about her."

I suggested the Earl's Court Exhibition, little thinking at the time what it was going to lead to; but the lady at first wouldn't hear of it, and the party at the next table calling for their bill (they had asked for it once or twice before, when I came to think of it), I had to go across to them.

When I got back the argument had just concluded, and the lady was holding up her finger.

"On condition that we leave at half-past nine, and that you go straight to Caxton Hall," she said.

"We'll see about it," said Mr. Parable, and offered me half a crown.

Tips being against the rules, I couldn't take it. Besides, one of the jumpers had his eye on me. I explained to him, jocosely, that I was doing it for a bet. He was surprised when I handed him his hat, but, the lady whispering to him, he remembered himself in time.

As they went out together I heard Mr. Parable say to the lady:

"It's funny what a shocking memory I have for names."

To which the lady replied:

"You'll think it funnier still to-morrow." And then she laughed.

Mr. Horton thought he would know the lady again. He puts down her age at about twenty-six, describing her—to use his own piquant expression—as "a bit of all right." She had brown eyes and a taking way with her.

Miss Ida Jenks, in charge of the Eastern Cigarette Kiosk at the Earl's Court Exhibition, gives the following particulars:

From where I generally stand I can easily command a view of the interior of the Victoria Hall; that is, of course, to say when the doors are open, as on a warm night is usually the case.

On the evening of Thursday, the twenty-seventh, it was fairly well occupied, but not to any great extent. One couple attracted my attention by reason of the gentleman's erratic steering. Had he been my partner I should have suggested a polka, the tango not being the sort of dance that can be picked up in an evening. What I mean to say is, that he struck me as being more willing than experienced. Some of the bumps she got would have made me cross; but we all have our fancies, and, so far as I could judge, they both appeared to be enjoying themselves. It was after the "Hitchy Koo" that they came outside.

The seat to the left of the door is popular by reason of its being partly screened by bushes, but by leaning forward a little it is quite possible for me to see what goes on there. They were the first couple out, having had a bad collision near the bandstand, so easily secured it. The gentleman was laughing.

There was something about him from the first that made me think I knew him, and when he took off his hat to wipe his head it came to me all of a sudden, he being the exact image of his effigy at Madame Tussaud's, which, by a curious coincidence, I happened to have visited with a friend that very afternoon. The lady was what some people would call good-looking, and others mightn't.

I was watching them, naturally a little interested. Mr. Parable, in helping the lady to adjust her cloak, drew her—it may have been by accident—towards him; and then it was that a florid gentleman with a short pipe in his mouth stepped forward and addressed the lady. He raised his hat and, remarking "Good evening," added that he hoped she was "having a pleasant time." His tone, I should explain, was sarcastic.

The young woman, whatever else may be said of her, struck me as behaving quite correctly. Replying to his salutation with a cold and distant bow, she rose, and, turning to Mr. Parable, observed that she thought it was perhaps time for them to be going.

The gentleman, who had taken his pipe from his mouth, said—again in a sarcastic tone—that he thought so too, and offered the lady his arm.

"I don't think we need trouble you," said Mr. Parable, and stepped between them.

To describe what followed I, being a lady, am hampered for words. I remember seeing Mr. Parable's hat go up into the air, and then the next moment the florid gentleman's head was lying on my counter smothered in cigarettes. I naturally screamed for the police, but the crowd was dead against me; and it was only after what I believe in technical language would be termed "the fourth round" that they appeared upon the scene.

The last I saw of Mr. Parable he was shaking a young constable who had lost his helmet, while three other policemen had hold of him from behind. The florid gentleman's hat I found on the floor of my kiosk and returned to him; but after a useless attempt to get it on his head, he disappeared with it in his hand. The lady was nowhere to be seen.

Miss Jenks thinks she would know her again. She was wearing a hat trimmed with black chiffon and a spray of poppies, and was slightly freckled.

Superintendent S. Wade, in answer to questions put to him by our representative, vouchsafed the following replies:

Yes. I was in charge at the Vine Street Police Station on the night of Thursday, the twenty-seventh.

No. I have no recollection of a charge of any description being preferred against any gentleman of the name of Parable.

Yes. A gentleman was brought in about ten o'clock charged with brawling at the Earl's Court Exhibition and assaulting a constable in the discharge of his duty.

The gentleman gave the name of Mr. Archibald Quincey, Harcourt Buildings, Temple.

No. The gentleman made no application respecting bail, electing to pass the night in the cells. A certain amount of discretion is permitted to us, and we made him as comfortable as possible.

Yes. A lady.

No. About a gentleman who had got himself into trouble at the Earl's Court Exhibition. She mentioned no name.

I showed her the charge sheet. She thanked me and went away.

That I cannot say. I can only tell you that at nine-fifteen on Friday morning bail was tendered, and, after inquiries, accepted in the person of Julius Addison Tupp, of the Sunnybrook Steam Laundry, Twickenham.

That is no business of ours.

The accused who, I had seen to it, had had a cup of tea and a little toast at seven-thirty, left in company with Mr. Tupp soon after ten.

Superintendent Wade admitted he had known cases where accused parties, to avoid unpleasantness, had stated their names to be other than their own, but declined to discuss the matter further.

Superintendent Wade, while expressing his regret that he had no more time to bestow upon our representative, thought it highly probable that he would know the lady again if he saw her.

Without professing to be a judge of such matters, Superintendent Wade thinks she might be described as a highly intelligent young woman, and of exceptionally prepossessing appearance.

From Mr. Julius Tupp, of the Sunnybrook Steam Laundry, Twickenham, upon whom our representative next called, we have been unable to obtain much assistance, Mr. Tupp replying to all questions put to him by the one formula, "Not talking."

Fortunately, our representative, on his way out through the drying ground, was able to obtain a brief interview with Mrs. Tupp.

Mrs. Tupp remembers admitting a young lady to the house on the morning of Friday, the twenty-eighth, when she opened the door to take in the milk. The lady, Mrs. Tupp remembers, spoke in a husky voice, the result, as the young lady explained with a pleasant laugh, of having passed the night wandering about Ham Common, she having been misdirected the previous evening by a fool of a railway porter, and not wishing to disturb the neighbourhood by waking people up at two o'clock in the morning, which, in Mrs. Tupp's opinion, was sensible of her.

Mrs. Tupp describes the young lady as of agreeable manners, but looking, naturally, a bit washed out. The lady asked for Mr. Tupp, explaining that a friend of his was in trouble, which did not in the least surprise Mrs. Tupp, she herself not holding with Socialists and such like. Mr. Tupp, on being informed, dressed hastily and went downstairs, and he and the young lady left the house together. Mr. Tupp, on being questioned as to the name of his friend, had called up that it was no one Mrs. Tupp would know, a Mr. Quince—it may have been Quincey.

Mrs. Tupp is aware that Mr. Parable is also a Socialist, and is acquainted with the saying about thieves hanging together. But has worked for Mr. Parable for years and has always found him a most satisfactory client; and, Mr. Tupp appearing at this point, our representative thanked Mrs. Tupp for her information and took his departure.

Mr. Horatius Condor, Junior, who consented to partake of luncheon in company with our representative at the Holborn Restaurant, was at first disinclined to be of much assistance, but eventually supplied our representative with the following information:

My relationship to Mr. Archibald Quincey, Harcourt Buildings, Temple, is perhaps a little difficult to define.

How he himself regards me I am never quite sure. There will be days together when we will be quite friendly like, and at other times he will be that offhanded and peremptory you might think I was his blooming office boy.

On Friday morning, the twenty-eighth, I didn't get to Harcourt Buildings at the usual time, knowing that Mr. Quincey would not be there himself, he having arranged to interview Mr. Parable for the Daily Chronicle at ten o'clock. I allowed him half an hour, to be quite safe, and he came in at a quarter past eleven.

He took no notice of me. For about ten minutes—it may have been less—he walked up and down the room, cursing and swearing and kicking the furniture about. He landed an occasional walnut table in the middle of my shins, upon which I took the opportunity of wishing him "Good morning," and he sort of woke up, as you might say.

"How did the interview go off?" I says. "Got anything interesting?"

"Yes," he says; "quite interesting. Oh, yes, decidedly interesting."

He was holding himself in, if you understand, speaking with horrible slowness and deliberation.

"D'you know where he was last night?" he asks me.

"Yes," I says; "Caxton Hall, wasn't it?—meeting to demand the release of Miss Clebb."

He leans across the table till his face was within a few inches of mine.

"Guess again," he says.

I wasn't doing any guessing. He had hurt me with the walnut table, and I was feeling a bit short-tempered.

"Oh! don't make a game of it," I says. "It's too early in the morning."

"At the Earl's Court Exhibition," he says; "dancing the tango with a lady that he picked up in St. James's Park."

"Well," I says, "why not? He don't often get much fun." I thought it best to treat it lightly.

He takes no notice of my observation.

"A rival comes upon the scene," he continues—"a fatheaded ass, according to my information—and they have a stand-up fight. He gets run in and spends the night in a Vine Street police cell."

I suppose I was grinning without knowing it.

"Funny, ain't it?" he says.

"Well," I says, "it has its humorous side, hasn't it? What'll he get?"

"I am not worrying about what *he* is going to get," he answers back. "I am worrying about what *I* am going to get."

I thought he had gone dotty.

"What's it got to do with you?" I says.

"If old Wotherspoon is in a good humour," he continues, "and the constable's head has gone down a bit between now and Wednesday, I may get off with forty shillings and a public reprimand.

"On the other hand," he goes on—he was working himself into a sort of fit—"if the constable's head goes on swelling, and old Wotherspoon's liver gets worse, I've got to be prepared for a month without the option. That is, if I am fool enough—"

He had left both the doors open, which in the daytime we generally do, our chambers being at the top. Miss Dorton—that's Mr. Parable's secretary—barges into the room. She didn't seem to notice me. She staggers to a chair and bursts into tears.

"He's gone," she says; "he's taken cook with him and gone."

"Gone!" says the guv'nor. "Where's he gone?"

"To Fingest," she says through her sobs—"to the cottage. Miss Bulstrode came in just after you had left," she says. "He wants to get away from everyone and have a few days' quiet. And then he is coming back, and he is going to do it himself."

"Do what?" says the guv'nor, irritable like.

"Fourteen days," she wails. "It'll kill him."

"But the case doesn't come on till Wednesday," says the guv'nor. "How do you know it's going to be fourteen days?"

"Miss Bulstrode," she says, "she's seen the magistrate. He says he always gives fourteen days in cases of unprovoked assault."

"But it wasn't unprovoked," says the guv'nor. "The other man began it by knocking off his hat. It was self-defence."

"She put that to him," she says, "and he agreed that that would alter his view of the case. But, you see," she continues, "we can't find the other man. He isn't likely to come forward of his own accord."

"The girl must know," says the guv'nor—"this girl he picks up in St. James's Park, and goes dancing with. The man must have been some friend of hers."

"But we can't find her either," she says. "He doesn't even know her name—he can't remember it."

"You will do it, won't you?" she says.

"Do what?" says the guv'nor again.

"The fourteen days," she says.

"But I thought you said he was going to do it himself?" he says.

"But he mustn't," she says. "Miss Bulstrode is coming round to see you. Think of it! Think of the headlines in the papers," she says. "Think of the Fabian Society. Think of the Suffrage cause. We mustn't let him."

"What about me?" says the guv'nor. "Doesn't anybody care for me?"

"You don't matter," she says. "Besides," she says, "with your influence you'll be able to keep it out of the papers. If it comes out that it was Mr. Parable, nothing on earth will be able to."

The guv'nor was almost as much excited by this time as she was.

"I'll see the Fabian Society and the Women's Vote and the Home for Lost Cats at Battersea, and all the rest of the blessed bag of tricks—"

I'd been thinking to myself, and had just worked it out.

"What's he want to take his cook down with him for?" I says.

"To cook for him," says the guv'nor. "What d'you generally want a cook for?"

"Rats!" I says. "Does he usually take his cook with him?"

"No," answered Miss Dorton. "Now I come to think of it, he has always hitherto put up with Mrs. Meadows."

"You will find the lady down at Fingest," I says, "sitting opposite him and enjoying a recherche dinner for two."

The guv'nor slaps me on the back, and lifts Miss Dorton out of her chair.

"You get on back," he says, "and telephone to Miss Bulstrode. I'll be round at half-past twelve."

Miss Dorton went out in a dazed sort of condition, and the guv'nor gives me a sovereign, and tells me I can have the rest of the day to myself.

Mr. Condor, Junior, considers that what happened subsequently goes to prove that he was right more than it proves that he was wrong.

Mr. Condor, Junior, also promised to send us a photograph of himself for reproduction, but, unfortunately, up to the time of going to press it had not arrived.

From Mrs. Meadows, widow of the late Corporal John Meadows, v.c., Turberville, Bucks, the following further particulars were obtained by our local representative:

I have done for Mr. Parable now for some years past, my cottage being only a mile off, which makes it easy for me to look after him.

Mr. Parable likes the place to be always ready so that he can drop in when he chooses, he sometimes giving me warning and sometimes not. It was about the end of last month—on a Friday, if I remember rightly—that he suddenly turned up.

As a rule, he walks from Henley station, but on this occasion he arrived in a fly, he having a young woman with him, and she having a bag—his cook, as he explained to me. As a rule, I do everything for Mr. Parable, sleeping in the cottage when he is there; but to tell the truth, I was glad to see her. I never was much of a cook myself, as my poor dead husband has remarked on more than one occasion, and I don't pretend to be. Mr. Parable added, apologetic like, that he had been suffering lately from indigestion.

"I am only too pleased to see her," I says. "There are the two beds in my room, and we shan't quarrel." She was quite a sensible young woman, as I had judged from the first look at her, though suffering at the time from a cold. She hires a bicycle from Emma Tidd, who only uses it on a Sunday, and, taking a market basket, off she starts for Henley, Mr. Parable saying he would go with her to show her the way.

They were gone a goodish time, which, seeing it's eight miles, didn't so much surprise me; and when they got back we all three had dinner together, Mr. Parable arguing that it made for what he called "labour saving." Afterwards I cleared away, leaving them talking together; and later on they had a walk round the garden, it being a moonlight night, but a bit too cold for my fancy.

In the morning I had a chat with her before he was down. She seemed a bit worried.

"I hope people won't get talking," she says. "He would insist on my coming."

"Well," I says, "surely a gent can bring his cook along with him to cook for him. And as for people talking, what I always say is, one may just as well give them something to talk about and save them the trouble of making it up."

"If only I was a plain, middle-aged woman," she says, "it would be all right."

"Perhaps you will be, all in good time," I says, but, of course, I could see what she was driving at. A nice, clean, pleasant-faced young woman she was, and not of the ordinary class. "Meanwhile," I says, "if you don't mind taking a bit of motherly advice, you might remember that your place is the kitchen, and his the parlour. He's a dear good man, I know, but human nature is human nature, and it's no good pretending it isn't."

She and I had our breakfast together before he was up, so that when he came down he had to have his alone, but afterwards she comes into the kitchen and closes the door.

"He wants to show me the way to High Wycombe," she says. "He will have it there are better shops at Wycombe. What ought I to do?"

My experience is that advising folks to do what they don't want to do isn't the way to do it.

"What d'you think yourself?" I asked her.

"I feel like going with him," she says, "and making the most of every mile."

And then she began to cry.

"What's the harm!" she says. "I have heard him from a dozen platforms ridiculing class distinctions. Besides," she says, "my people have been farmers for generations. What was Miss Bulstrode's father but a grocer? He ran a hundred shops instead of one. What difference does that make?"

"When did it all begin?" I says. "When did he first take notice of you like?"

"The day before yesterday," she answers. "He had never seen me before," she says. "I was just 'Cook'—something in a cap and apron that he passed occasionally on the stairs. On Thursday he saw me in my best clothes, and fell in love with me. He doesn't know it himself, poor dear, not yet, but that's what he's done."

Well, I couldn't contradict her, not after the way I had seen him looking at her across the table.

"What are your feelings towards him," I says, "to be quite honest? He's rather a good catch for a young person in your position."

"That's my trouble," she says. "I can't help thinking of that. And then to be 'Mrs. John Parable'! That's enough to turn a woman's head."

"He'd be a bit difficult to live with," I says.

"Geniuses always are," she says; "it's easy enough if you just think of them as children. He'd be a bit fractious at times, that's all. Underneath, he's just the kindest, dearest—"

"Oh, you take your basket and go to High Wycombe," I says. "He might do worse."

I wasn't expecting them back soon, and they didn't come back soon. In the afternoon a motor stops at the gate, and out of it steps Miss Bulstrode, Miss Dorton—that's the young lady that writes for him—and Mr. Quincey. I told them I couldn't say when he'd be back, and they said it didn't matter, they just happening to be passing.

"Did anybody call on him yesterday?" asks Miss Bulstrode, careless like—"a lady?"

"No," I says; "you are the first as yet."

"He's brought his cook down with him, hasn't he?" says Mr. Quincey.

"Yes," I says, "and a very good cook too," which was the truth.

"I'd like just to speak a few words with her," says Miss Bulstrode.

"Sorry, m'am," I says, "but she's out at present; she's gone to Wycombe."

"Gone to Wycombe!" they all says together.

"To market," I says. "It's a little farther, but, of course, it stands to reason the shops there are better."

They looked at one another.

"That settles it," says Mr. Quincey. "Delicacies worthy to be set before her not available nearer than Wycombe, but must be had. There's going to be a pleasant little dinner here to-night."

"The hussy!" says Miss Bulstrode, under her breath.

They whispered together for a moment, then they turns to me.

"Good afternoon, Mrs. Meadows," says Mr. Quincey. "You needn't say we called. He wanted to be alone, and it might vex him."

I said I wouldn't, and I didn't. They climbed back into the motor and went off.

Before dinner I had call to go into the woodshed. I heard a scuttling as I opened the door. If I am not mistaken, Miss Dorton was hiding in the corner where we keep the coke. I didn't see any good in making a fuss, so I left her there. When I got back to the kitchen, cook asked me if we'd got any parsley.

"You'll find a bit in the front," I says, "to the left of the gate," and she went out. She came back looking scared.

"Anybody keep goats round here?" she asked me.

"Not that I know of, nearer than Ibstone Common," I says.

"I could have sworn I saw a goat's face looking at me out of the gooseberry bushes while I was picking the parsley," she says. "It had a beard."

"It's the half light," I says. "One can imagine anything."

"I do hope I'm not getting nervy," she says.

I thought I'd have another look round, and made the excuse that I wanted a pail of water. I was stooping over the well, which is just under the mulberry tree, when something fell close to me and lodged upon the bricks. It was a hairpin. I fixed the cover carefully upon the well in case of accident, and when I got in I went round myself and was careful to see that all the curtains were drawn.

Just before we three sat down to dinner again I took cook aside.

"I shouldn't go for any stroll in the garden to-night," I says. "People from the village may be about, and we don't want them gossiping." And she thanked me.

Next night they were there again. I thought I wouldn't spoil the dinner, but mention it afterwards. I saw to it again that the curtains were drawn, and slipped the catch of both the doors. And just as well that I did.

I had always heard that Mr. Parable was an amusing speaker, but on previous visits had not myself noticed it. But this time he seemed ten years younger than I had ever known him before; and during dinner, while we were talking and laughing quite merry like, I had the feeling more than once that people were meandering about outside. I had just finished clearing away, and cook was making the coffee, when there came a knock at the door.

"Who's that?" says Mr. Parable. "I am not at home to anyone."

"I'll see," I says. And on my way I slipped into the kitchen.

"Coffee for one, cook," I says, and she understood. Her cap and apron were hanging behind the door. I flung them across to her, and she caught them; and then I opened the front door.

They pushed past me without speaking, and went straight into the parlour. And they didn't waste many words on him either.

"Where is she?" asked Miss Bulstrode.

"Where's who?" says Mr. Parable.

"Don't lie about it," said Miss Bulstrode, making no effort to control herself. "The hussy you've been dining with?"

"Do you mean Mrs. Meadows?" says Mr. Parable.

I thought she was going to shake him.

"Where have you hidden her?" she says.

It was at that moment cook entered with the coffee.

If they had taken the trouble to look at her they might have had an idea. The tray was trembling in her hands, and in her haste and excitement she had put on her cap the wrong way round. But she kept control of her voice, and asked if she should bring some more coffee.

"Ah, yes! You'd all like some coffee, wouldn't you?" says Mr. Parable. Miss Bulstrode did not reply, but Mr. Quincey said he was cold and would like it. It was a nasty night, with a thin rain.

"Thank you, sir," says cook, and we went out together.

Cottages are only cottages, and if people in the parlour persist in talking loudly, people in the kitchen can't very well help overhearing.

There was a good deal of talk about "fourteen days," which Mr. Parable said he was going to do himself, and which Miss Dorton said he mustn't, because, if he did, it would be a victory for the enemies of humanity. Mr. Parable said something about "humanity," which I didn't rightly hear, but, whatever it was, it started Miss Dorton crying; and Miss Bulstrode called Mr. Parable a "blind Samson," who had had his hair cut by a designing minx who had been hired to do it.

It was all French to me, but cook was drinking in every word, and when she returned from taking them in their coffee she made no bones about it, but took up her place at the door with her ear to the keyhole.

It was Mr. Quincey who got them all quiet, and then he began to explain things. It seemed that if they could only find a certain gentleman and persuade him to come forward and acknowledge that he began a row, that then all would be well. Mr. Quincey would be fined forty shillings, and Mr. Parable's name would never appear. Failing that, Mr. Parable, according to Mr. Quincey, could do his fourteen days himself.

"I've told you once," says Mr. Parable, "and I tell you again, that I don't know the man's name, and can't give it you."

"We are not asking you to," says Mr. Quincey. "You give us the name of your tango partner, and we'll do the rest."

I could see cook's face; I had got a bit interested myself, and we were both close to the door. She hardly seemed to be breathing.

"I am sorry," says Mr. Parable, speaking very deliberate-like, "but I am not going to have her name dragged into this business."

"It wouldn't be," says Mr. Quincey. "All we want to get out of her is the name and address of the gentleman who was so anxious to see her home."

"Who was he?" says Miss Bulstrode. "Her husband?"

"No," says Mr. Parable; "he wasn't."

"Then who was he?" says Miss Bulstrode. "He must have been something to her—fiancé?"

"I am going to do the fourteen days myself," says Mr. Parable. "I shall come out all the fresher after a fortnight's complete rest and change."

Cook leaves the door with a smile on her face that made her look quite beautiful, and, taking some paper from the dresser drawer, began to write a letter.

They went on talking in the other room for another ten minutes, and then Mr. Parable lets them out himself, and goes a little way with them. When he came back we could hear him walking up and down the other room.

She had written and stamped the envelope; it was lying on the table.

"'Joseph Onions, Esq.,'" I says, reading the address. "'Auctioneer and House Agent, Broadway, Hammersmith.' Is that the young man?"

"That is the young man," she says, folding her letter and putting it in the envelope.

"And was he your fiancé?" I asked.

"No," she says. "But he will be if he does what I'm telling him to do."

"And what about Mr. Parable?" I says.

"A little joke that will amuse him later on," she says, slipping a cloak on her shoulders. "How once he nearly married his cook."

"I shan't be a minute," she says. And, with the letter in her hand, she slips out.

Mrs. Meadows, we understand, has expressed indignation at our publication of this interview, she being under the impression that she was simply having a friendly gossip with a neighbour. Our representative, however, is sure he explained to Mrs. Meadows that his visit was official; and, in any case, our duty to the public must be held to exonerate us from all blame in the matter.

Mr. Joseph Onions, of the Broadway, Hammersmith, auctioneer and house agent, expressed himself to our representative as most surprised at the turn that events had subsequently taken. The letter that Mr. Onions received from Miss Comfort Price was explicit and definite. It was to the effect that if he would call upon a certain Mr. Quincey, of Harcourt Buildings, Temple, and acknowledge that it was he who began the row at the Earl's Court Exhibition on the evening of the twenty-seventh, that then the engagement between himself and Miss Price, hitherto unacknowledged by the lady, might be regarded as a fact.

Mr. Onions, who describes himself as essentially a business man, decided before complying with Miss Price's request to take a few preliminary steps. As the result of judiciously conducted inquiries, first at the Vine Street Police Station, and secondly at Twickenham, Mr. Onions arrived later in the day at Mr. Quincey's chambers, with, to use his own expression, all the cards in his hand. It was Mr. Quincey who, professing himself unable to comply with Mr. Onion's suggestion, arranged the interview with Miss Bulstrode. And it was Miss Bulstrode herself who, on condition that Mr. Onions added to the undertaking the further condition that he would marry Miss Price before the end of the month, offered to make it two hundred. It was in their joint interest—Mr. Onions regarding himself and Miss Price as now one—that Mr. Onions suggested her making it three, using such arguments as, under the circumstances, naturally occurred to him—as, for example, the damage caused to the lady's reputation by the whole proceedings, culminating in a night spent by the lady, according to her own account, on Ham Common. That the price demanded was reasonable Mr. Onions considers as proved by Miss Bulstrode's eventual acceptance of his terms. That, having got out of him all that he wanted, Mr. Quincey should have "considered it his duty" to communicate the entire details of the transaction to Miss Price, through the medium of Mr. Andrews, thinking it "as well she should know the character of the man she proposed to marry," Mr. Onions considers a gross breach of etiquette as between gentlemen; and having regard to Miss Price's after behaviour, Mr. Onions can only say that she is not the girl he took her for.

Mr. Aaron Andrews, on whom our representative called, was desirous at first of not being drawn into the matter; but on our representative explaining to him that our only desire was to contradict false rumours likely to be harmful to Mr. Parable's reputation, Mr. Andrews saw the necessity of putting our representative in possession of the truth.

She came back on Tuesday afternoon, explained Mr. Andrews, and I had a talk with her.

"It is all right, Mr. Andrews," she told me; "they've been in communication with my young man, and Miss Bulstrode has seen the magistrate privately. The case will be dismissed with a fine of forty shillings, and Mr. Quincey has arranged to keep it out of the papers."

"Well, all's well that ends well," I answered; "but it might have been better, my girl, if you had mentioned that young man of yours a bit earlier."

"I did not know it was of any importance," she explained. "Mr. Parable told me nothing. If it hadn't been for chance, I should never have known what was happening."

I had always liked the young woman. Mr. Quincey had suggested my waiting till after Wednesday. But there seemed to me no particular object in delay.

"Are you fond of him?" I asked her.

"Yes," she answered. "I am fonder than—" And then she stopped herself suddenly and flared scarlet. "Who are you talking about?" she demanded.

"This young man of yours," I said. "Mr.—What's his name—Onions?"

"Oh, that?" she answered. "Oh, yes; he's all right."

"And if he wasn't?" I said, and she looked at me hard.

"I told him," she said, "that if he would do what I asked him to do, I'd marry him. And he seems to have done it."

"There are ways of doing everything," I said; and, seeing it wasn't going to break her heart, I told her just the plain facts. She listened without a word, and when I had finished she put her arms round my neck and kissed me. I am old enough to be her grandfather, but twenty years ago it might have upset me.

"I think I shall be able to save Miss Bulstrode that three hundred pounds," she laughed, and ran upstairs and changed her things. When later I looked into the kitchen she was humming.

Mr. John came up by the car, and I could see he was in one of his moods.

"Pack me some things for a walking tour," he said. "Don't forget the knapsack. I am going to Scotland by the eight-thirty."

"Will you be away long?" I asked him.

"It depends upon how long it takes me," he answered. "When I come back I am going to be married."

"Who is the lady?" I asked, though, of course, I knew.

"Miss Bulstrode," he said.

"Well," I said, "she—"

"That will do," he said; "I have had all that from the three of them for the last two days. She is a Socialist, and a Suffragist, and all the rest of it, and my ideal helpmate. She is well off, and that will enable me to devote all my time to putting the world to rights without bothering about anything else. Our home will be the nursery of advanced ideas. We shall share together the joys and delights of the public platform. What more can any man want?"

"You will want your dinner early," I said, "if you are going by the eight-thirty. I had better tell cook—"

He interrupted me again.

"You can tell cook to go to the devil," he said.

I naturally stared at him.

"She is going to marry a beastly little rotter of a rent collector that she doesn't care a damn for," he went on.

I could not understand why he seemed so mad about it.

"I don't see, in any case, what it's got to do with you," I said, "but, as a matter of fact, she isn't."

"Isn't what?" he said, stopping short and turning on me.

"Isn't going to marry him," I answered.

"Why not?" he demanded.

"Better ask her," I suggested.

I didn't know at the time that it was a silly thing to say, and I am not sure that I should not have said it if I had. When he is in one of his moods I always seem to get into one of mine. I have looked after Mr. John ever since he was a baby, so that we do not either of us treat the other quite as perhaps we ought to.

"Tell cook I want her," he said.

"She is just in the middle—" I began.

"I don't care where she is," he said. He seemed determined never to let me finish a sentence. "Send her up here."

She was in the kitchen by herself.

"He wants to see you at once," I said.

"Who does?" she asked.

"Mr. John," I said.

"What's he want to see me for?" she asked.

"How do I know?" I answered.

"But you do," she said. She always had an obstinate twist in her, and, feeling it would save time, I told her what had happened.

"Well," I said, "aren't you going?"

She was standing stock still staring at the pastry she was making. She turned to me, and there was a curious smile about her lips.

"Do you know what you ought to be wearing?" she said. "Wings, and a little bow and arrow."

She didn't even think to wipe her hands, but went straight upstairs. It was about half an hour later when the bell rang. Mr. John was standing by the window.

"Is that bag ready?" he said.

"It will be," I said.

I went out into the hall and returned with the clothes brush.

"What are you going to do?" he said.

"Perhaps you don't know it," I said, "but you are all over flour."

"Cook's going with me to Scotland," he said.

I have looked after Mr. John ever since he was a boy. He was forty-two last birthday, but when I shook hands with him through the cab window I could have sworn he was twenty-five again.

THE LESSON

The first time I met him, to my knowledge, was on an evil-smelling, one-funnelled steam boat that in those days plied between London Bridge and Antwerp. He was walking the deck arm-in-arm with a showily dressed but decidedly attractive young woman; both of them talking and laughing loudly. It struck me as odd, finding him a fellow-traveller by such a route. The passage occupied eighteen hours, and the first-class return fare was one pound twelve and six, including three meals each way; drinks, as the contract was careful to explain, being extra. I was earning thirty shillings a week at the time as clerk with a firm of agents in Fenchurch Street. Our business was the purchasing of articles on commission for customers in India, and I had learned to be a judge of values. The beaver lined coat he was wearing—for the evening, although it was late summer, was chilly—must have cost him a couple of hundred pounds, while his carelessly displayed jewellery he could easily have pawned for a thousand or more.

I could not help staring at him, and once, as they passed, he returned my look.

After dinner, as I was leaning with my back against the gunwale on the starboard side, he came out of the only private cabin that the vessel boasted, and taking up a position opposite to me, with his legs well apart and a big cigar between his thick lips, stood coolly regarding me, as if appraising me.

"Treating yourself to a little holiday on the Continent?" he inquired.

I had not been quite sure before he spoke, but his lisp, though slight, betrayed the Jew. His features were coarse, almost brutal; but the restless eyes were so brilliant, the whole face so suggestive of power and character, that, taking him as a whole, the feeling he inspired was admiration, tempered by fear. His tone was one of kindly contempt—the tone of a man accustomed to find most people his inferiors, and too used to the discovery to be conceited about it.

Behind it was a note of authority that it did not occur to me to dispute.

"Yes," I answered, adding the information that I had never been abroad before, and had heard that Antwerp was an interesting town.

"How long have you got?" he asked.

"A fortnight," I told him.

"Like to see a bit more than Antwerp, if you could afford it, wouldn't you?" he suggested. "Fascinating little country Holland. Just long enough—a fortnight—to do the whole of it. I'm a Dutchman, a Dutch Jew."

"You speak English just like an Englishman," I told him. It was somehow in my mind to please him. I could hardly have explained why.

"And half a dozen other languages equally well," he answered, laughing. "I left Amsterdam when I was eighteen as steerage passenger in an emigrant ship. I haven't seen it since."

He closed the cabin door behind him, and, crossing over, laid a strong hand on my shoulder.

"I will make a proposal to you," he said. "My business is not of the kind that can be put out of mind, even for a few days, and there are reasons"—he glanced over his shoulder towards the cabin door, and gave vent to a short laugh—"why I did not want to bring any of my own staff with me. If you care for a short tour, all expenses paid at slap-up hotels and a ten-pound note in your pocket at the end, you can have it for two hours' work a day."

I suppose my face expressed my acceptance, for he did not wait for me to speak.

"Only one thing I stipulate for," he added, "that you mind your own business and keep your mouth shut. You're by yourself, aren't you?"

"Yes," I told him.

He wrote on a sheet of his notebook, and, tearing it out, handed it to me.

"That's your hotel at Antwerp," he said. "You are Mr. Horatio Jones's secretary." He chuckled to himself as he repeated the name, which certainly did not fit him. "Knock at my sitting-room door at nine o'clock tomorrow morning. Good night!"

He ended the conversation as abruptly as he had begun it, and returned to his cabin.

I got a glimpse of him next morning, coming out of the hotel bureau. He was speaking to the manager in French, and had evidently given instructions concerning me, for I found myself preceded by an obsequious waiter to quite a charming bedroom on the second floor, while the "English breakfast" placed before me later in the coffee-room was of a size and character that in those days I did not often enjoy. About the work, also, he was as good as his word. I was rarely occupied for more than two hours each morning. The duties consisted chiefly of writing letters and sending off telegrams. The letters he signed and had posted himself, so that I never learnt his real name—not during that fortnight—but I gathered enough to be aware that he was a man whose business interests must have been colossal and world-wide.

He never introduced me to "Mrs. Horatio Jones," and after a few days he seemed to be bored with her, so that often I would take her place as his companion in afternoon excursions.

I could not help liking the man. Strength always compels the adoration of youth; and there was something big and heroic about him. His daring, his swift decisions, his utter unscrupulousness, his occasional cruelty when necessity seemed to demand it. One could imagine him in earlier days a born leader of savage hordes, a lover of fighting for its own sake, meeting all obstacles with fierce welcome, forcing his way onward, indifferent to the misery and destruction caused by his progress, his eyes never swerving from their goal; yet not without a sense of rough justice, not altogether without kindliness when it could be indulged in without danger.

One afternoon he took me with him into the Jewish quarter of Amsterdam, and threading his way without hesitation through its maze of unsavoury slums, paused before a narrow three-storeyed house overlooking a stagnant backwater.

"The room I was born in," he explained. "Window with the broken pane on the second floor. It has never been mended."

I stole a glance at him. His face betrayed no suggestion of sentiment, but rather of amusement. He offered me a cigar, which I was glad of, for the stench from the offal-laden water behind us was distracting, and for a while we both smoked in silence: he with his eyes half-closed; it was a trick of his when working out a business problem.

"Curious, my making such a choice," he remarked. "A butcher's assistant for my father and a consumptive buttonhole-maker for my mother. I suppose I knew what I was about. Quite the right thing for me to have done, as it turned out."

I stared at him, wondering whether he was speaking seriously or in grim jest. He was given at times to making odd remarks. There was a vein of the fantastic in him that was continually cropping out and astonishing me.

"It was a bit risky," I suggested. "Better choose something a little safer next time."

He looked round at me sharply, and, not quite sure of his mood, I kept a grave face.

"Perhaps you are right," he agreed, with a laugh. "We must have a talk about it one day."

After that visit to the Goortgasse he was less reserved with me, and would often talk to me on subjects that I should never have guessed would have interested him. I found him a curious mixture. Behind the shrewd, cynical man of business I caught continual glimpses of the visionary.

I parted from him at The Hague. He paid my fare back to London, and gave me an extra pound for travelling expenses, together with the ten-pound note he had promised me. He had packed off "Mrs. Horatio Jones" some days before, to the relief, I imagine, of both of them, and he himself continued his journey to Berlin. I never expected to see him again, although for the next few months I often thought of him, and even tried to discover him by inquiries in the City. I had, however, very little to go upon, and after I had left Fenchurch Street behind me, and drifted into literature, I forgot him.

Until one day I received a letter addressed to the care of my publishers. It bore the Swiss postmark, and opening it and turning to the signature I sat wondering for the moment where I had met "Horatio Jones." And then I remembered.

He was lying bruised and broken in a woodcutter's hut on the slopes of the Jungfrau. Had been playing a fool's trick, so he described it, thinking he could climb mountains at his age. They would carry him down to Lauterbrunnen as soon as he could be moved farther with safety, but for the present he had no one to talk to but the nurse and a Swiss doctor who climbed up to see him every third day. He begged me, if I could spare the time, to come over and spend a week with him. He enclosed a hundred-pound cheque for my expenses, making no apology for doing so. He was complimentary about my first book, which he had been reading, and asked me to telegraph him my reply, giving me his real name, which, as I had guessed it would, proved to be one of the best known in the financial world. My time was my own now, and I wired him that I would be with him the following Monday.

He was lying in the sun outside the hut when I arrived late in the afternoon, after a three-hours' climb followed by a porter carrying my small amount of luggage. He could not raise his hand, but his strangely brilliant eyes spoke their welcome.

"I am glad you were able to come," he said. "I have no near relations, and my friends—if that is the right term—are business men who would be bored to tears. Besides, they are not the people I feel I want to talk to, now."

He was entirely reconciled to the coming of death. Indeed, there were moments when he gave me the idea that he was looking forward to it with an awed curiosity. With the conventional notion of cheering him, I talked of staying till he was able to return with me to civilisation, but he only laughed.

"I am not going back," he said. "Not that way. What they may do afterwards with these broken bones does not much concern either you or me.

"It's a good place to die in," he continued. "A man can think up here."

It was difficult to feel sorry for him, his own fate appearing to make so little difference to himself. The world was still full of interest to him—not his own particular corner of it: that, he gave me to understand, he had tidied up and dismissed from his mind. It was the future, its coming problems, its possibilities, its new developments, about which he seemed eager to talk. One might have imagined him a young man with the years before him.

One evening—it was near the end—we were alone together. The woodcutter and his wife had gone down into the valley to see their children, and the nurse, leaving him in my charge, had gone for a walk. We had carried him round to his favourite side of the hut facing the towering mass of the Jungfrau. As the shadows lengthened it seemed to come nearer to us, and there fell a silence upon us.

Gradually I became aware that his piercing eyes were fixed on me, and in answer I turned and looked at him.

"I wonder if we shall meet again," he said, "or, what is more important, if we shall remember one another."

I was puzzled for the moment. We had discussed more than once the various religions of mankind, and his attitude towards the orthodox beliefs had always been that of amused contempt.

"It has been growing upon me these last few days," he continued. "It flashed across me the first time I saw you on the boat. We were fellow-students. Something, I don't know what, drew us very close together. There was a woman. They were burning her. And then there was a rush of people and a sudden darkness, and your eyes close to mine."

I suppose it was some form of hypnotism, for, as he spoke, his searching eyes fixed on mine, there came to me a dream of narrow streets filled with a strange crowd, of painted houses such as I had never seen, and a haunting fear that seemed to be always lurking behind each shadow. I shook myself free, but not without an effort.

"So that's what you meant," I said, "that evening in the Goortgasse. You believe in it?"

"A curious thing happened to me," he said, "when I was a child. I could hardly have been six years old. I had gone to Ghent with my parents. I think it was to visit some relative. One day we went into the castle. It was in ruins then, but has since been restored. We were in what was once the council chamber. I stole away by myself to the other end of the great room and, not knowing why I did so, I touched a spring concealed in the masonry, and a door swung open with a harsh, grinding noise. I remember peering round the opening. The others had their backs towards me, and I slipped through and closed the door behind me. I seemed instinctively to know my way. I ran down a flight of steps and along dark corridors through which I had to feel my way with my hands, till I came to a small door in an angle of the wall. I knew the room that lay the other side. A photograph was taken of it and published years afterwards, when the place was discovered, and it was exactly as I knew it with its way out underneath the city wall through one of the small houses in the Aussermarkt.

"I could not open the door. Some stones had fallen against it, and fearing to get punished, I made my way back into the council room. It was empty when I reached it. They were searching for me in the other rooms, and I never told them of my adventure."

At any other time I might have laughed. Later, recalling his talk that evening, I dismissed the whole story as mere suggestion, based upon the imagination of a child; but at the time those strangely brilliant eyes had taken possession of me. They remained still fixed upon me as I sat on the low rail of the veranda watching his white face, into which the hues of death seemed already to be creeping.

I had a feeling that, through them, he was trying to force remembrance of himself upon me. The man himself—the very soul of him—seemed to be concentrated in them. Something formless and yet distinct was visualising itself before me. It came to me as a physical relief when a spasm of pain caused him to turn his eyes away from me.

"You will find a letter when I am gone," he went on, after a moment's silence. "I thought that you might come too late, or that I might not have strength enough to tell you. I felt that out of the few people I have met outside business, you would be the most likely not to dismiss the matter as mere nonsense. What I am glad of myself, and what I wish you to remember, is that I am dying with all my faculties about me. The one thing I have always feared through life was old age, with its gradual mental decay. It has always seemed to me that I have died more or less suddenly while still in possession of my will. I have always thanked God for that."

He closed his eyes, but I do not think he was sleeping; and a little later the nurse returned, and we carried him indoors. I had no further conversation with him, though at his wish during the following two days I continued to read to him, and on the third day he died.

I found the letter he had spoken of. He had told me where it would be. It contained a bundle of banknotes which he was giving me—so he wrote—with the advice to get rid of them as quickly as possible.

"If I had not loved you," the letter continued, "I would have left you an income, and you would have blessed me, instead of cursing me, as you should have done, for spoiling your life."

This world was a school, so he viewed it, for the making of men; and the one thing essential to a man was strength. One gathered the impression of a deeply religious man. In these days he would, no doubt, have been claimed as a theosophist; but his beliefs he had made for, and adapted to, himself—to his vehement, conquering temperament. God needed men to serve Him—to help Him. So, through many changes, through many ages, God gave men life: that by contest and by struggle they might ever increase in strength; to those who proved themselves most fit the sterner task, the humbler beginnings, the greater obstacles. And the crown of well-doing was ever victory. He appeared to have convinced himself that he was one of the chosen, that he was destined for great ends. He had been a slave in the time of the Pharaohs; a priest in Babylon; had clung to the swaying ladders in the sack of Rome; had won his way into the councils when Europe was a battlefield of contending tribes; had climbed to power in the days of the Borgias.

To most of us, I suppose, there come at odd moments haunting thoughts of strangely familiar, far-off things; and one wonders whether they are memories or dreams. We dismiss them as we grow older and the present with its crowding interests shuts them out; but in youth they were more persistent. With him they appeared to have remained, growing in reality. His recent existence, closed under the white sheet in the hut behind me as I read, was only one chapter of the story; he was looking forward to the next.

He wondered, so the letter ran, whether he would have any voice in choosing it. In either event he was curious of the result. What he anticipated confidently were new opportunities, wider experience. In what shape would these come to him?

The letter ended with a strange request. It was that, on returning to England, I should continue to think of him: not of the dead man I had known, the Jewish banker, the voice familiar to me, the trick of speech, of manner—all such being but the changing clothes—but of the man himself, the soul of him, that would seek and perhaps succeed in revealing itself to me.

A postscript concluded the letter, to which at the time I attached no importance. He had made a purchase of the hut in which he had died. After his removal it was to remain empty.

I folded the letter and placed it among other papers, and passing into the hut took a farewell glance at the massive, rugged face. The mask might have served a sculptor for the embodiment of strength. He gave one the feeling that having conquered death he was sleeping.

I did what he had requested of me. Indeed, I could not help it. I thought of him constantly. That may have been the explanation of it.

I was bicycling through Norfolk, and one afternoon, to escape a coming thunderstorm, I knocked at the door of a lonely cottage on the outskirts of a common. The woman, a kindly bustling person, asked me in; and hoping I would excuse her, as she was busy ironing, returned to her work in another room. I thought myself alone, and was standing at the window watching the pouring rain. After a while, without knowing why, I turned. And then I saw a child seated on a high chair behind a table in a dark corner of the room. A book of pictures was open before it, but it was looking at me. I could hear the sound of the woman at her ironing in the other room. Outside there was the steady thrashing of the rain. The child was looking at me with large, round eyes filled with a terrible pathos. I noticed that the little body was misshapen. It never moved; it made no sound; but I had the feeling that out of those strangely wistful eyes something was trying to speak to me. Something was forming itself before me—not visible to my sight; but it was there, in the room. It was the man I had last looked upon as, dying, he sat beside me in the hut below the Jungfrau. But something had happened to him. Moved by instinct I went over to him and lifted him out of his chair, and with a sob the little wizened arms closed round my neck and he clung to me crying—a pitiful, low, wailing cry.

Hearing his cry, the woman came back. A comely, healthy-looking woman. She took him from my arms and comforted him.

"He gets a bit sorry for himself at times," she explained. "At least, so I fancy. You see, he can't run about like other children, or do anything without getting pains."

"Was it an accident?" I asked.

"No," she answered, "and his father as fine a man as you would find in a day's march. Just a visitation of God, as they tell me. Sure I don't know why. There never was a better little lad, and clever, too, when he's not in pain. Draws wonderfully."

The storm had passed. He grew quieter in her arms, and when I had promised to come again and bring him a new picture-book, a little grateful smile flickered across the drawn face, but he would not talk.

I kept in touch with him. Mere curiosity would have made me do that. He grew more normal as the years went by, and gradually the fancy that had come to me at our first meeting faded farther into the background. Sometimes, using the very language of the dead man's letter, I would talk to him, wondering if by any chance some flash of memory would come back to him, and once or twice it seemed to me that into the mild, pathetic eyes there came a look that I had seen before, but it passed away, and indeed, it was difficult to think of this sad little human oddity, with its pleading helplessness, in connection with the strong, swift, conquering spirit that I had watched passing away amid the silence of the mountains.

The one thing that brought joy to him was his art. I cannot help thinking that, but for his health, he would have made a name for himself. His work was always clever and original, but it was the work of an invalid.

"I shall never be great," he said to me once. "I have such wonderful dreams, but when it comes to working them out there is something that hampers me. It always seems to me as if at the last moment a hand was stretched out that clutched me by the feet. I long so, but I have not the strength. It is terrible to be one of the weaklings."

It clung to me, that word he had used. For a man to know he is weak; it sounds a paradox, but a man must be strong to know that. And dwelling upon this, and upon his patience and his gentleness, there came to me suddenly remembrance of that postscript, the significance of which I had not understood.

He was a young man of about three-or four-and-twenty at the time. His father had died, and he was living in poor lodgings in the south of London, supporting himself and his mother by strenuous, ill-paid work.

"I want you to come with me for a few days' holiday," I told him.

I had some difficulty in getting him to accept my help, for he was very proud in his sensitive, apologetic way. But I succeeded eventually, persuading him it would be good for his work. Physically the journey must have cost him dear, for he could never move his body without pain, but the changing landscapes and the strange cities more than repaid him; and when one morning I woke him early and he saw for the first time the distant mountains clothed in dawn, there came a new light into his eyes.

We reached the hut late in the afternoon. I had made my arrangements so that we should be there alone. Our needs were simple, and in various wanderings I had learnt to be independent. I did not tell him why I had brought him there, beyond the beauty and stillness of the place. Purposely I left him much alone there, making ever-lengthening walks my excuse, and though he was always glad of my return I felt that the desire was growing upon him to be there by himself.

One evening, having climbed farther than I had intended, I lost my way. It was not safe in that neighbourhood to try new pathways in the dark, and chancing upon a deserted shelter, I made myself a bed upon the straw.

I found him seated outside the hut when I returned, and he greeted me as if he had been expecting me just at that moment and not before. He guessed just what had happened, he told me, and had not been alarmed. During the day I found him watching me, and in the evening, as we sat in his favourite place outside the hut, he turned to me.

"You think it true?" he said. "That you and I sat here years ago and talked?"

"I cannot tell," I answered. "I only know that he died here, if there be such a thing as death—that no one has ever lived here since. I doubt if the door has ever been opened till we came."

"They have always been with me," he continued, "these dreams. But I have always dismissed them. They seemed so ludicrous. Always there came to me wealth, power, victory. Life was so easy."

He laid his thin hand on mine. A strange new look came into his eyes—a look of hope, almost of joy.

"Do you know what it seems to me?" he said. "You will laugh perhaps, but the thought has come to me up here that God has some fine use for me. Success was making me feeble. He has given me weakness and failure that I may learn strength. The great thing is to be strong."

SYLVIA OF THE LETTERS

Old Ab Herrick, so most people called him. Not that he was actually old; the term was an expression of liking rather than any reflection on his years. He lived in an old-fashioned house—old-fashioned, that is, for New York—on the south side of West Twentieth Street: once upon a time, but that was long ago, quite a fashionable quarter. The house, together with Mrs. Travers, had been left him by a maiden aunt. An "apartment" would, of course, have been more suitable to a bachelor of simple habits, but the situation was convenient from a journalistic point of view, and for fifteen years Abner Herrick had lived and worked there.

Then one evening, after a three days' absence, Abner Herrick returned to West Twentieth Street, bringing with him a little girl wrapped up in a shawl, and a wooden box tied with a piece of cord. He put the box on the table; and the young lady, loosening her shawl, walked to the window and sat down facing the room.

Mrs. Travers took the box off the table and put it on the floor—it was quite a little box—and waited.

"This young lady," explained Abner Herrick, "is Miss Ann Kavanagh, daughter of—of an old friend of mine."

"Oh!" said Mrs. Travers, and remained still expectant.

"Miss Kavanagh," continued Abner Herrick, "will be staying with us for—" He appeared to be uncertain of the length of Miss Kavanagh's visit. He left the sentence unfinished and took refuge in more pressing questions.

"What about the bedroom on the second floor? Is it ready? Sheets aired—all that sort of thing?"

"It can be," replied Mrs. Travers. The tone was suggestive of judgment reserved.

"I think, if you don't mind, Mrs. Travers, that we'd like to go to bed as soon as possible." From force of habit Abner S. Herrick in speaking employed as a rule the editorial "we." "We have been travelling all day and we are very tired. To-morrow morning—"

"I'd like some supper," said Miss Kavanagh from her seat in the window, without moving.

"Of course," agreed Miss Kavanagh's host, with a feeble pretence that the subject had been on the tip of his tongue. As a matter of fact, he really had forgotten all about it. "We might have it up here while the room is being got ready. Perhaps a little—"

"A soft boiled egg and a glass of milk, if you please, Mrs. Travers," interrupted Miss Kavanagh, still from her seat at the window.

"I'll see about it," said Mrs. Travers, and went out, taking the quite small box with her.

Such was the coming into this story of Ann Kavanagh at the age of eight years; or, as Miss Kavanagh herself would have explained, had the question been put to her, eight years and seven months, for Ann Kavanagh was a precise young lady. She was not beautiful—not then. She was much too sharp featured; the little pointed chin protruding into space to quite a dangerous extent. Her large dark eyes were her one redeeming feature. But the level brows above them were much too ready with their frown. A sallow complexion and nondescript hair deprived her of that charm of colouring on which youth can generally depend for attraction, whatever its faults of form. Nor could it truthfully be said that sweetness of disposition afforded compensation.

"A self-willed, cantankerous little imp I call her," was Mrs. Travers's comment, expressed after one of the many trials of strength between them, from which Miss Kavanagh had as usual emerged triumphant.

"It's her father," explained Abner Herrick, feeling himself unable to contradict.

"It's unfortunate," answered Mrs. Travers, "whatever it is."

To Uncle Ab himself, as she had come to call him, she could on occasion be yielding and affectionate; but that, as Mrs. Travers took care to point out to her, was a small thing to her credit.

"If you had the instincts of an ordinary Christian child," explained Mrs. Travers to her, "you'd be thinking twenty-four hours a day of what you could do to repay him for all his loving kindness to you; instead of causing him, as you know you do, a dozen heartaches in a week. You're an ungrateful little monkey, and when he's gone you'll—"

Upon which Miss Kavanagh, not waiting to hear more, flew upstairs and, locking herself in her own room, gave herself up to howling and remorse; but was careful not to emerge until she felt bad tempered again; and able, should opportunity present itself, to renew the contest with Mrs. Travers unhampered by sentiment.

But Mrs. Travers's words had sunk in deeper than that good lady herself had hoped for; and one evening, when Abner Herrick was seated at his desk penning a scathing indictment of the President for lack of firmness and decision on the tariff question, Ann, putting her thin arms round his neck and rubbing her little sallow face against his right-hand whisker, took him to task on the subject.

"You're not bringing me up properly—not as you ought to," explained Ann. "You give way to me too much, and you never scold me."

"Not scold you!" exclaimed Abner with a certain warmth of indignation. "Why, I'm doing it all—"

"Not what *I* call scolding," continued Ann. "It's very wrong of you. I shall grow up horrid if you don't help me."

As Ann with great clearness pointed out to him, there was no one else to undertake the job with any chance of success. If Abner failed her, then she supposed there was no hope for her: she would end by becoming a wicked woman, and everybody, including herself, would hate her. It was a sad prospect. The contemplation of it brought tears to Ann's eyes.

He saw the justice of her complaint and promised to turn over a new leaf. He honestly meant to do so; but, like many another repentant sinner, found himself feeble before the difficulties of performance. He might have succeeded better had it not been for her soft deep eyes beneath her level brows.

"You're not much like your mother," so he explained to her one day, "except about the eyes. Looking into your eyes I can almost see your mother."

He was smoking a pipe beside the fire, and Ann, who ought to have been in bed, had perched herself upon one of the arms of his chair and was kicking a hole in the worn leather with her little heels.

"She was very beautiful, my mother, wasn't she?" suggested Ann.

Abner Herrick blew a cloud from his pipe and watched carefully the curling smoke.

"In a way, yes," he answered. "Quite beautiful."

"What do you mean, 'In a way'?" demanded Ann with some asperity.

"It was a spiritual beauty, your mother's," Abner explained. "The soul looking out of her eyes. I don't think it possible to imagine a more beautiful disposition than your mother's. Whenever I think of your mother," continued Abner after a pause, "Wordsworth's lines always come into my mind."

He murmured the quotation to himself, but loud enough to be heard by sharp ears. Miss Kavanagh was mollified.

"You were in love with my mother, weren't you?" she questioned him kindly.

"Yes, I suppose I was," mused Abner, still with his gaze upon the curling smoke.

"What do you mean by 'you suppose you were'?" snapped Ann. "Didn't you know?"

The tone recalled him from his dreams.

"I was in love with your mother very much," he corrected himself, turning to her with a smile.

"Then why didn't you marry her?" asked Ann. "Wouldn't she have you?"

"I never asked her," explained Abner.

"Why not?" persisted Ann, returning to asperity.

He thought a moment.

"You wouldn't understand," he told her.

"Yes, I would," retorted Ann.

"No, you wouldn't," he contradicted her quite shortly. They were both beginning to lose patience with one another. "No woman ever could."

"I'm not a woman," explained Ann, "and I'm very smart. You've said so yourself."

"Not so smart as all that," growled Abner. "Added to which, it's time for you to go to bed."

Her anger with him was such that it rendered her absolutely polite. It had that occasional effect upon her. She slid from the arm of his chair and stood beside him, a rigid figure of frozen femininity.

"I think you are quite right, Uncle Herrick. Good night!" But at the door she could not resist a parting shot:

"You might have been my father, and then perhaps she wouldn't have died. I think it was very wicked of you."

After she was gone Abner sat gazing into the fire, and his pipe went out. Eventually the beginnings of a smile stole to the corners of his mouth, but before it could spread any farther he dismissed it with a sigh.

Abner, for the next day or two, feared a renewal of the conversation, but Ann appeared to have forgotten it; and as time went by it faded from Abner's own memory. Until one evening quite a while later.

The morning had brought him his English mail. It had been arriving with some regularity, and Ann had noticed that Abner always opened it before his other correspondence. One letter he read through twice, and Ann, who was pretending to be reading the newspaper, felt that he was looking at her.

"I have been thinking, my dear," said Abner, "that it must be rather lonely for you here, all by yourself."

"It would be," answered Ann, "if I were here all by myself."

"I mean," said Abner, "without any other young person to talk to and—and to play with."

"You forget," said Ann, "that I'm nearly thirteen."

"God bless my soul," said Abner. "How time does fly!"

"Who is she?" asked Ann.

"It isn't a 'she,'" explained Abner. "It's a 'he.' Poor little chap lost his mother two years ago, and now his father's dead. I thought—it occurred to me we might put him up for a time. Look after him a bit. What do you think? It would make the house more lively, wouldn't it?"

"It might," said Ann.

She sat very silent, and Abner, whose conscience was troubling him, watched her a little anxiously. After a time she looked up.

"What's he like?" she asked.

"Precisely what I am wondering myself," confessed Abner. "We shall have to wait and see. But his mother—his mother," repeated Abner, "was the most beautiful woman I have ever known. If he is anything like she was as a girl—" He left the sentence unfinished.

"You have not seen her since—since she was young?" questioned Ann.

Abner shook his head. "She married an Englishman. He took her back with him to London."

"I don't like Englishmen," said Ann.

"They have their points," suggested Abner. "Besides, boys take after their mothers, they say." And Abner rose and gathered his letters together.

Ann remained very thoughtful all that day. In the evening, when Abner for a moment laid down his pen for the purpose of relighting his pipe, Ann came to him, seating herself on the corner of the desk.

"I suppose," she said, "that's why you never married mother?"

Abner's mind at the moment was much occupied with the Panama Canal.

"What mother?" he asked. "Whose mother?"

"My mother," answered Ann. "I suppose men are like that."

"What are you talking about?" said Abner, dismissing altogether the Panama Canal.

"You loved my mother very much," explained Ann with cold deliberation. "She always made you think of Wordsworth's perfect woman."

"Who told you all that?" demanded Abner.

"You did."

"I did?"

"It was the day you took me away from Miss Carew's because she said she couldn't manage me," Ann informed him.

"Good Lord! Why, that must be two years ago," mused Abner.

"Three," Ann corrected him. "All but a few days."

"I wish you'd use your memory for things you're wanted to remember," growled Abner.

"You said you had never asked her to marry you," pursued Ann relentlessly; "you wouldn't tell me why. You said I shouldn't understand."

"My fault," muttered Abner. "I forget you're a child. You ask all sorts of questions that never ought to enter your head, and I'm fool enough to answer you."

One small tear that had made its escape unnoticed by her was stealing down her cheek. He wiped it away and took one of her small paws in both his hands.

"I loved your mother very dearly," he said gravely. "I had loved her from a child. But no woman will ever understand the power that beauty has upon a man. You see we're built that way. It's Nature's lure. Later on, of course, I might have forgotten; but then it was too late. Can you forgive me?"

"But you still love her," reasoned Ann through her tears, "or you wouldn't want him to come here."

"She had such a hard time of it," pleaded Abner. "It made things easier to her, my giving her my word that I would always look after the boy. You'll help me?"

"I'll try," said Ann. But there was not much promise in the tone.

Nor did Matthew Pole himself, when he arrived, do much to help matters. He was so hopelessly English. At least, that was the way Ann put it. He was shy and sensitive. It is a trying combination. It made him appear stupid and conceited. A lonely childhood had rendered him unsociable, unadaptable. A dreamy, imaginative temperament imposed upon him long moods of silence: a liking for long solitary walks. For the first time Ann and Mrs. Travers were in agreement.

"A sulky young dog," commented Mrs. Travers. "If I were your uncle I'd look out for a job for him in San Francisco."

"You see," said Ann in excuse for him, "it's such a foggy country, England. It makes them like that."

"It's a pity they can't get out of it," said Mrs. Travers.

Also, sixteen is an awkward age for a boy. Virtues, still in the chrysalis state, are struggling to escape from their parent vices. Pride, an excellent quality making for courage and patience, still appears in the swathings of arrogance. Sincerity still expresses itself in the language of rudeness. Kindness itself is apt to be mistaken for amazing impertinence and love of interference.

It was kindness—a genuine desire to be useful, that prompted him to point out to Ann her undoubted faults and failings, nerved him to the task of bringing her up in the way she should go. Mrs. Travers had long since washed her hands of the entire business. Uncle Ab, as Matthew also called him, had proved himself a weakling. Providence, so it seemed to Matthew, must have been waiting impatiently for his advent. Ann at first thought it was some new school of humour. When she found he was serious she set herself to cure him. But she never did. He was too conscientious for that. The instincts of the guide, philosopher, and friend to humanity in general were already too strong in him. There were times when Abner almost wished that Matthew Pole senior had lived a little longer.

But he did not lose hope. At the back of his mind was the fancy that these two children of his loves would come together. Nothing is quite so sentimental as a healthy old bachelor. He pictured them making unity from his confusions; in imagination heard the patter on the stairs of tiny feet. To all intents and purposes he would be a grandfather. Priding himself on his cunning, he kept his dream to himself, as he thought, but under-estimated Ann's smartness.

For days together she would follow Matthew with her eyes, watching him from behind her long lashes, listening in silence to everything he said, vainly seeking to find points in him. He was unaware of her generous intentions. He had a vague feeling he was being criticised. He resented it even in those days.

"I do try," said Ann suddenly one evening apropos of nothing at all. "No one will ever know how hard I try not to dislike him."

Abner looked up.

"Sometimes," continued Ann, "I tell myself I have almost succeeded. And then he will go and do something that will bring it all on again."

"What does he do?" asked Abner.

"Oh, I can't tell you," confessed Ann. "If I told you it would sound as if it was my fault. It's all so silly. And then he thinks such a lot of himself. If one only knew why! He can't tell you himself when you ask him."

"You have asked him?" queried Abner.

"I wanted to know," explained Ann. "I thought there might be something in him that I could like."

"Why do you want to like him?" asked Abner, wondering how much she had guessed.

"I know," wailed Ann. "You are hoping that when I am grown up I shall marry him. And I don't want to. It's so ungrateful of me."

"Well, you're not grown up yet," Abner consoled her. "And so long as you are feeling like that about it, I'm not likely to want you to marry him."

"It would make you so happy," sobbed Ann.

"Yes, but we've got to think of the boy, don't forget that," laughed Abner. "Perhaps he might object."

"He would. I know he would," cried Ann with conviction. "He's no better than I am."

"Have you been asking him to?" demanded Abner, springing up from his chair.

"Not to marry me," explained Ann. "But I told him he must be an unnatural little beast not to try to like me when he knew how you loved me."

"Helpful way of putting it," growled Abner. "And what did he say to that?"

"Admitted it," flashed Ann indignantly. "Said he had tried."

Abner succeeded in persuading her that the path of dignity and virtue lay in her dismissing the whole subject from her mind.

He had made a mistake, so he told himself. Age may be attracted by contrast, but youth has no use for its opposite. He would send Matthew away. He could return for week-ends. Continually so close to one another, they saw only one another's specks and flaws; there is no beauty without perspective. Matthew wanted the corners rubbed off him, that was all. Mixing more with men, his priggishness would be laughed out of him. Otherwise he was quite a decent youngster, clean minded, high principled. Clever, too: he often said quite unexpected things. With approaching womanhood, changes were taking place in Ann. Seeing her every day one hardly noticed them; but there were times when, standing before him flushed from a walk or bending over him to kiss him before starting for some friendly dance, Abner would blink his eyes and be puzzled. The thin arms were growing round and firm; the sallow complexion warming into olive; the once patchy, mouse-coloured hair darkening into a rich harmony of brown. The eyes beneath her level brows, that had always been her charm, still reminded Abner of her mother; but there was more light in them, more danger.

"I'll run down to Albany and talk to Jephson about him," decided Abner. "He can come home on Saturdays."

The plot might have succeeded: one never can tell. But a New York blizzard put a stop to it. The cars broke down, and Abner, walking home in thin shoes from a meeting, caught a chill, which, being neglected, proved fatal.

Abner was troubled as he lay upon his bed. The children were sitting very silent by the window. He sent Matthew out on a message, and then beckoned Ann to come to him. He loved the boy, too, but Ann was nearer to him.

"You haven't thought any more," he whispered, "about—"

"No," answered Ann. "You wished me not to."

"You must never think," he said, "to show your love for my memory by doing anything that would not make you happy. If I am anywhere around," he continued with a smile, "it will be your good I shall be watching for, not my own way. You will remember that?"

He had meant to do more for them, but the end had come so much sooner than he had expected. To Ann he left the house (Mrs. Travers had already retired on a small pension) and a sum that, judiciously invested, the friend and attorney thought should be sufficient for her needs, even supposing—The friend and attorney, pausing to dwell upon the oval face with its dark eyes, left the sentence unfinished.

To Matthew he wrote a loving letter, enclosing a thousand dollars. He knew that Matthew, now in a position to earn his living as a journalist, would rather have taken nothing. It was to be looked upon merely as a parting gift. Matthew decided to spend it on travel. It would fit him the better for his journalistic career, so he explained to Ann. But in his heart he had other ambitions. It would enable him to put them to the test.

So there came an evening when Ann stood waving a handkerchief as a great liner cast its moorings. She watched it till its lights grew dim, and then returned to West Twentieth Street. Strangers would take possession of it on the morrow. Ann had her supper in the kitchen in company with the nurse, who had stayed on at her request; and that night, slipping noiselessly from her room, she lay upon the floor, her head resting against the arm of the chair where Abner had been wont to sit and smoke his evening pipe; somehow it seemed to comfort her. And Matthew the while, beneath the stars, was pacing the silent deck of the great liner and planning out the future.

To only one other being had he ever confided his dreams. She lay in the churchyard; and there was nothing left to encourage him but his own heart. But he had no doubts. He would be a great writer. His two hundred pounds would support him till he had gained a foothold. After that he would climb swiftly. He had done right, so he told himself, to turn his back on journalism: the grave of literature. He would see men and cities, writing as he went. Looking back, years later, he was able to congratulate himself on having chosen the right road. He thought it would lead him by easy ascent to fame and fortune. It did better for him than that. It led him through poverty and loneliness, through hope deferred and heartache—through long nights of fear, when pride and confidence fell upon him, leaving him only the courage to endure.

His great poems, his brilliant essays, had been rejected so often that even he himself had lost all love for them. At the suggestion of an editor more kindly than the general run, and urged by need, he had written some short pieces of a less ambitious nature. It was in bitter disappointment he commenced them, regarding them as mere pot-boilers. He would not give them his name. He signed them "Aston Rowant." It was the name of the village in Oxfordshire where he had been born. It occurred to him by chance. It would serve the purpose as well as another. As the work progressed it grew upon him. He made his stories out of incidents and people he had seen; everyday comedies and tragedies that he had lived among, of things that he had felt; and when after their appearance in the magazine a publisher was found willing to make them into a book, hope revived in him.

It was but short-lived. The few reviews that reached him contained nothing but ridicule. So he had no place even as a literary hack!

He was living in Paris at the time in a noisy, evil-smelling street leading out of the Quai Saint-Michel. He thought of Chatterton, and would loaf on the bridges looking down into the river where the drowned lights twinkled.

And then one day there came to him a letter, sent on to him from the publisher of his one book. It was signed "Sylvia," nothing else, and bore no address. Matthew picked up the envelope. The postmark was "London, s.e."

It was a childish letter. A prosperous, well-fed genius, familiar with such, might have smiled at it. To Matthew in his despair it brought healing. She had found the book lying in an empty railway carriage; and undeterred by moral scruples had taken it home with her. It had remained forgotten for a time, until when the end really seemed to have come her hand by chance had fallen on it. She fancied some kind little wandering spirit—the spirit perhaps of someone who had known what it was to be lonely and very sad and just about broken almost—must have manoeuvred the whole thing. It had seemed to her as though some strong and gentle hand had been laid upon her in the darkness. She no longer felt friendless. And so on.

The book, he remembered, contained a reference to the magazine in which the sketches had first appeared. She would be sure to have noticed this. He would send her his answer. He drew his chair up to the flimsy table, and all that night he wrote.

He did not have to think. It came to him, and for the first time since the beginning of things he had no fear of its not being accepted. It was mostly about himself, and the rest was about her, but to most of those who read it two months later it seemed to be about themselves. The editor wrote a charming letter, thanking him for it; but at the time the chief thing that worried him was whether "Sylvia" had seen it. He waited anxiously for a few weeks, and then received her second letter. It was a more womanly letter than the first. She had understood the story, and her words of thanks almost conveyed to him the flush of pleasure with which she had read it. His friendship, she confessed, would be very sweet to her, and still more delightful the thought that he had need of her: that she also had something to give. She would write, as he wished, her real thoughts and feelings. They would never know one another, and that would give her boldness. They would be comrades, meeting only in dreamland.

In this way commenced the whimsical romance of Sylvia and Aston Rowant; for it was too late now to change the name—it had become a name to conjure with. The stories, poems, and essays followed now in regular succession. The anxiously expected letters reached him in orderly procession. They grew in interest, in helpfulness. They became the letters of a wonderfully sane, broad-minded, thoughtful woman—a woman of insight, of fine judgment. Their praise was rare enough to be precious. Often they would contain just criticism, tempered by sympathy, lightened by humour. Of her troubles, sorrows, fears, she came to write less and less, and even then not until they were past and she could laugh at them. The subtlest flattery she gave him was the suggestion that he had taught her to put these things into their proper place. Intimate, self-revealing as her letters were, it was curious he never shaped from them any satisfactory image of the writer.

A brave, kind, tender woman. A self-forgetting, quickly-forgiving woman. A many-sided woman, responding to joy, to laughter: a merry lady, at times. Yet by no means a perfect woman. There could be flashes of temper, one felt that; quite often occasional unreasonableness; a tongue that could be cutting. A sweet, restful, greatly loving woman, but still a woman: it would be wise to remember that. So he read her from her letters. But herself, the eyes, and hair, and lips of her, the voice and laugh and smile of her, the hands and feet of her, always they eluded him.

He was in Alaska one spring, where he had gone to collect material for his work, when he received the last letter she ever wrote him. They neither of them knew then it would be the last. She was leaving London, so the postscript informed him, sailing on the following Saturday for New York, where for the future she intended to live.

It worried him that postscript. He could not make out for a long time why it worried him. Suddenly, in a waste of endless snows, the explanation flashed across him. Sylvia of the letters was a living woman! She could travel—with a box, he supposed, possibly with two or three, and parcels. Could take tickets, walk up a gangway, stagger about a deck feeling, maybe, a little seasick. All these years he had been living with her in dreamland she had been, if he had only known it, a Miss Somebody-or-other, who must have stood every morning in front of a looking-glass with hairpins in her mouth. He had never thought of her doing these things; it shocked him. He could not help feeling it was indelicate of her—coming to life in this sudden, uncalled-for manner.

He struggled with this new conception of her, and had almost forgiven her, when a further and still more startling suggestion arrived to plague him. If she really lived why should he not see her, speak to her? So long as she had remained in her hidden temple, situate in the vague recesses of London, s.e., her letters had contented him. But now that she had moved, now that she was no longer a voice but a woman! Well, it would be interesting to see what she was like. He imagined the introduction: "Miss Somebody-or-other, allow me to present you to Mr. Matthew Pole." She would have no idea he was Aston Rowant. If she happened to be young, beautiful, in all ways satisfactory, he would announce himself. How astonished, how delighted she would be.

But if not! If she were elderly, plain? The wisest, wittiest of women have been known to have an incipient moustache. A beautiful spirit can, and sometimes does, look out of goggle eyes. Suppose she suffered from indigestion and had a shiny nose! Would her letters ever again have the same charm for him? Absurd that they should not. But would they?

The risk was too great. Giving the matter long and careful consideration, he decided to send her back into dreamland.

But somehow she would not go back into dreamland, would persist in remaining in New York, a living, breathing woman.

Yet even so, how could he find her? He might, say, in a poem convey to her his desire for a meeting. Would she comply? And if she did, what would be his position, supposing the inspection to result unfavourably for her? Could he, in effect, say to her: "Thank you for letting me have a look at you; that is all I wanted. Good-bye"?

She must, she should remain in dreamland. He would forget her postscript; in future throw her envelopes unglanced at into the wastepaper basket. Having by this simple exercise of his will replaced her in London, he himself started for New York—on his way back to Europe, so he told himself. Still, being in New York, there was no reason for not lingering there a while, if merely to renew old memories.

Of course, if he had really wanted to find Sylvia it would have been easy from the date upon the envelope to have discovered the ship "sailing the following Saturday." Passengers were compelled to register their names in full, and to state their intended movements after arrival in America. Sylvia was not a common Christian name. By the help of a five-dollar bill or two—. The idea had not occurred to him before. He dismissed it from his mind and sought a quiet hotel up town.

New York was changed less than he had anticipated. West Twentieth Street in particular was precisely as, leaning out of the cab window, he had looked back upon it ten years ago. Business had more and more taken possession of it, but had not as yet altered its appearance. His conscience smote him as he turned the corner that he had never once written to Ann. He had meant to, it goes without saying, but during those first years of struggle and failure his pride had held him back. She had always thought him a fool; he had felt she did. He would wait till he could write to her of success, of victory. And then when it had slowly, almost imperceptibly, arrived—! He wondered why he never had. Quite a nice little girl, in some respects. If only she had been less conceited, less self-willed. Also rather a pretty girl she had shown signs of becoming. There were times—He remembered an evening before the lamps were lighted. She had fallen asleep curled up in Abner's easy chair, one small hand resting upon the arm. She had always had quite attractive hands—a little too thin. Something had moved him to steal across softly without waking her. He smiled at the memory.

And then her eyes, beneath the level brows! It was surprising how Ann was coming back to him. Perhaps they would be able to tell him, the people of the house, what had become of her. If they were decent people they would let him wander round a while. He would explain that he had lived there in Abner Herrick's time. The room where they had sometimes been agreeable to one another while Abner, pretending to read, had sat watching them out of the corner of an eye. He would like to sit there for a few moments, by himself.

He forgot that he had rung the bell. A very young servant had answered the door and was staring at him. He would have walked in if the small servant had not planted herself deliberately in his way. It recalled him to himself.

"I beg pardon," said Matthew, "but would you please tell me who lives here?"

The small servant looked him up and down with growing suspicion.

"Miss Kavanagh lives here," she said. "What do you want?"

The surprise was so great it rendered him speechless. In another moment the small servant would have slammed the door.

"Miss Ann Kavanagh?" he inquired, just in time.

"That's her name," admitted the small servant, less suspicious.

"Will you please tell her Mr. Pole—Mr. Matthew Pole," he requested.

"I'll see first if she is in," said the small servant, and shut the door.

It gave Matthew a few minutes to recover himself, for which he was glad. Then the door opened again suddenly.

"You are to come upstairs," said the small servant.

It sounded so like Ann that it quite put him at his ease. He followed the small servant up the stairs.

"Mr. Matthew Pole," she announced severely, and closed the door behind him.

Ann was standing by the window and came to meet him. It was in front of Abner's empty chair that they shook hands.

"So you have come back to the old house," said Matthew.

"Yes," she answered. "It never let well. The last people who had it gave it up at Christmas. It seemed the best thing to do, even from a purely economical point of view.

"What have you been doing all these years?" she asked him.

"Oh, knocking about," he answered. "Earning my living." He was curious to discover what she thought of Matthew, first of all.

"It seems to have agreed with you," she commented, with a glance that took him in generally, including his clothes.

"Yes," he answered. "I have had more luck than perhaps I deserved."

"I am glad of that," said Ann.

He laughed. "So you haven't changed so very much," he said. "Except in appearance.

"Isn't that the most important part of a woman?" suggested Ann.

"Yes," he answered, thinking. "I suppose it is."

She was certainly very beautiful.

"How long are you stopping in New York?" she asked him.

"Oh, not long," he explained.

"Don't leave it for another ten years," she said, "before letting me know what is happening to you. We didn't get on very well together as children; but we mustn't let him think we're not friends. It would hurt him."

She spoke quite seriously, as if she were expecting him any moment to open the door and join them. Involuntarily Matthew glanced round the room. Nothing seemed altered. The worn carpet, the faded curtains, Abner's easy chair, his pipe upon the corner of the mantelpiece beside the vase of spills.

"It is curious," he said, "finding this vein of fancy, of tenderness in you. I always regarded you as such a practical, unsentimental young person."

"Perhaps we neither of us knew each other too well, in those days," she answered.

The small servant entered with the tea.

"What have you been doing with yourself?" he asked, drawing his chair up to the table.

She waited till the small servant had withdrawn.

"Oh, knocking about," she answered. "Earning my living."

"It seems to have agreed with you," he repeated, smiling.

"It's all right now," she answered. "It was a bit of a struggle at first."

"Yes," he agreed. "Life doesn't temper the wind to the human lamb. But was there any need in your case?" he asked. "I thought—"

"Oh, that all went," she explained. "Except the house."

"I'm sorry," said Matthew. "I didn't know."

"Oh, we have been a couple of pigs," she laughed, replying to his thoughts. "I did sometimes think of writing you. I kept the address you gave me. Not for any assistance; I wanted to fight it out for myself. But I was a bit lonely."

"Why didn't you?" he asked.

She hesitated for a moment.

"It's rather soon to make up one's mind," she said, "but you seem to me to have changed. Your voice sounds so different. But as a boy—well, you were a bit of a prig, weren't you? I imagined you writing me good advice and excellent short sermons. And it wasn't that that I was wanting."

"I think I understand," he said. "I'm glad you got through.

"What is your line?" he asked. "Journalism?"

"No," she answered. "Too self-opinionated."

She opened a bureau that had always been her own and handed him a programme. "Miss Ann Kavanagh, Contralto," was announced on it as one of the chief attractions.

"I didn't know you had a voice," said Matthew.

"You used to complain of it," she reminded him.

"Your speaking voice," he corrected her. "And it wasn't the quality of that I objected to. It was the quantity."

She laughed.

"Yes, we kept ourselves pretty busy bringing one another up," she admitted.

They talked a while longer: of Abner and his kind, quaint ways; of old friends. Ann had lost touch with most of them. She had studied singing in Brussels, and afterwards her master had moved to London and she had followed him. She had only just lately returned to New York.

The small servant entered to clear away the tea things. She said she thought that Ann had rung. Her tone implied that anyhow it was time she had. Matthew rose and Ann held out her hand.

"I shall be at the concert," he said.

"It isn't till next week," Ann reminded him.

"Oh, I'm not in any particular hurry," said Matthew. "Are you generally in of an afternoon?"

"Sometimes," said Ann.

He thought as he sat watching her from his stall that she was one of the most beautiful women he had ever seen. Her voice was not great. She had warned him not to expect too much.

"It will never set the Thames on fire," she had said. "I thought at first that it would. But such as it is I thank God for it."

It was worth that. It was sweet and clear and had a tender quality.

Matthew waited for her at the end. She was feeling well disposed towards all creatures and accepted his suggestion of supper with gracious condescension.

He had called on her once or twice during the preceding days. It was due to her after his long neglect of her, he told himself, and had found improvement in her. But to-night she seemed to take a freakish pleasure in letting him see that there was much of the old Ann still left in her: the frank conceit of her; the amazing self-opinionatedness of her; the waywardness, the wilfulness, the unreasonableness of her; the general uppishness and dictatorialness of her; the contradictoriness and flat impertinence of her; the swift temper and exasperating tongue of her.

It was almost as if she were warning him. "You see, I am not changed, except, as you say, in appearance. I am still Ann with all the old faults and failings that once made life in the same house with me a constant trial to you. Just now my very imperfections appear charms. You have been looking at the sun—at the glory of my face, at the wonder of my arms and hands. Your eyes are blinded. But that will pass. And underneath I am still Ann. Just Ann."

They had quarrelled in the cab on the way home. He forgot what it was about, but Ann had said some quite rude things, and her face not being there in the darkness to excuse her, it had made him very angry. She had laughed again on the steps, and they had shaken hands. But walking home through the still streets Sylvia had plucked at his elbow.

What fools we mortals be—especially men! Here was a noble woman—a restful, understanding, tenderly loving woman; a woman as nearly approaching perfection as it was safe for a woman to go! This marvellous woman was waiting for him with outstretched arms (why should he doubt it?)—and just because Nature had at last succeeded in making a temporary success of Ann's skin and had fashioned a rounded line above her shoulder-blade! It made him quite cross with himself. Ten years ago she had been gawky and sallow-complexioned. Ten years hence she might catch the yellow jaundice and lose it all. Passages in Sylvia's letters returned to him. He remembered that far-off evening in his Paris attic when she had knocked at his door with her great gift of thanks. Recalled how her soft shadow hand had stilled his pain. He spent the next two days with Sylvia. He re-read all her letters, lived again the scenes and moods in which he had replied to them.

Her personality still defied the efforts of his imagination, but he ended by convincing himself that he would know her when he saw her.

But counting up the women on Fifth Avenue towards whom he had felt instinctively drawn, and finding that the number had already reached eleven, began to doubt his intuition. On the morning of the third day he met Ann by chance in a bookseller's shop. Her back was towards him. She was glancing through Aston Rowant's latest volume.

"What I," said the cheerful young lady who was attending to her, "like about him is that he understands women so well."

"What I like about him," said Ann, "is that he doesn't pretend to."

"There's something in that," agreed the cheerful young lady. "They say he's here in New York."

Ann looked up.

"So I've been told," said the cheerful young lady.

"I wonder what he's like?" said Ann.

"He wrote for a long time under another name," volunteered the cheerful young lady. "He's quite an elderly man."

It irritated Matthew. He spoke without thinking.

"No, he isn't," he said. "He's quite young."

The ladies turned and looked at him.

"You know him?" queried Ann. She was most astonished, and appeared disbelieving. That irritated him further.

"If you care about it," he said. "I will introduce you to him."

Ann made no answer. He bought a copy of the book for himself, and they went out together. They turned towards the park.

Ann seemed thoughtful. "What is he doing here in New York?" she wondered.

"Looking for a lady named Sylvia," answered Matthew.

He thought the time was come to break it to her that he was a great and famous man. Then perhaps she would be sorry she had said what she had said in the cab. Seeing he had made up his mind that his relationship to her in the future would be that of an affectionate brother, there would be no harm in also letting her know about Sylvia. That also might be good for her.

They walked two blocks before Ann spoke. Matthew, anticipating a pleasurable conversation, felt no desire to hasten matters.

"How intimate are you with him?" she demanded. "I don't think he would have said that to a mere acquaintance."

"I'm not a mere acquaintance," said Matthew. "I've known him a long time."

"You never told me," complained Ann.

"Didn't know it would interest you," replied Matthew.

He waited for further questions, but they did not come. At Thirty-fourth Street he saved her from being run over and killed, and again at Forty-second Street. Just inside the park she stopped abruptly and held out her hand.

"Tell him," she replied, "that if he is really serious about finding Sylvia, I may—I don't say I can—but I may be able to help him."

He did not take her hand, but stood stock still in the middle of the path and stared at her.

"You!" he said. "You know her?"

She was prepared for his surprise. She was also prepared—not with a lie, that implies evil intention. Her only object was to have a talk with the gentleman and see what he was like before deciding on her future proceedings—let us say, with a plausible story.

"We crossed on the same boat," she said. "We found there was a good deal in common between us. She—she told me things." When you came to think it out it was almost the truth.

"What is she like?" demanded Matthew.

"Oh, just—well, not exactly—" It was an awkward question. There came to her relief the reflection that there was really no need for her to answer it.

"What's it got to do with you?" she said.

"I am Aston Rowant," said Matthew.

The Central Park, together with the universe in general, fell away and disappeared. Somewhere out of chaos was sounding a plaintive voice: "What is she like? Can't you tell me? Is she young or old?"

It seemed to have been going on for ages. She made one supreme gigantic effort, causing the Central Park to reappear, dimly, faintly, but it was there again. She was sitting on a seat. Matthew—Aston Rowant, whatever it was—was seated beside her.

"You've seen her? What is she like?"

"I can't tell you."

He was evidently very cross with her. It seemed so unkind of him.

"Why can't you tell me—or, why won't you tell me? Do you mean she's too awful for words?"

"No, certainly not—as a matter of fact—"

"Well, what?"

She felt she must get away or there would be hysterics somewhere. She sprang up and began to walk rapidly towards the gate. He followed her.

"I'll write you," said Ann.

"But why—?"

"I can't," said Ann. "I've got a rehearsal."

A car was passing. She made a dash for it and clambered on. Before he could make up his mind it had gathered speed.

Ann let herself in with her key. She called downstairs to the small servant that she wasn't to be disturbed for anything. She locked the door.

So it was to Matthew that for six years she had been pouring out her inmost thoughts and feelings! It was to Matthew that she had laid bare her tenderest, most sacred dreams! It was at Matthew's feet that for six years she had been sitting, gazing up with respectful admiration, with reverential devotion! She recalled her letters, almost passage for passage, till she had to hold her hands to her face to cool it. Her indignation, one might almost say fury, lasted till tea-time.

In the evening—it was in the evening time that she had always written to him—a more reasonable frame of mind asserted itself. After all, it was hardly his fault. He couldn't have known who she was. He didn't know now. She had wanted to write. Without doubt he had helped her, comforted her loneliness; had given her a charming friendship, a delightful comradeship. Much of his work had been written for her, to her. It was fine work. She had been proud of her share in it. Even allowing there were faults—irritability, shortness of temper, a tendency to bossiness!—underneath it all was a man. The gallant struggle, the difficulties overcome, the long suffering, the high courage—all that she, reading between the lines, had divined of his life's battle! Yes, it was a man she had worshipped. A woman need not be ashamed of that. As Matthew he had seemed to her conceited, priggish. As Aston Rowant she wondered at his modesty, his patience.

And all these years he had been dreaming of her; had followed her to New York; had—

There came a sudden mood so ludicrous, so absurdly unreasonable that Ann herself stopped to laugh at it. Yet it was real, and it hurt. He had come to New York thinking of Sylvia, yearning for Sylvia. He had come to New York with one desire: to find Sylvia. And the first pretty woman that had come across his path had sent Sylvia clean out of his head. There could be no question of that. When Ann Kavanagh stretched out her hand to him in that very room a fortnight ago he had stood before her dazzled, captured. From that moment Sylvia had been tossed aside and forgotten. Ann Kavanagh could have done what she liked with him. She had quarrelled with him that evening of the concert. She had meant to quarrel with him.

And then for the first time he had remembered Sylvia. That was her reward—Sylvia's: it was Sylvia she was thinking of—for six years' devoted friendship; for the help, the inspiration she had given him.

As Sylvia, she suffered from a very genuine and explainable wave of indignant jealousy. As Ann, she admitted he ought not to have done it, but felt there was excuse for him. Between the two she feared her mind would eventually give way. On the morning of the second day she sent Matthew a note asking him to call in the afternoon. Sylvia might be there, or she might not. She would mention it to her.

She dressed herself in a quiet, dark-coloured frock. It seemed un-committal and suitable to the occasion. It also happened to be the colour that best suited her. She would not have the lamps lighted.

Matthew arrived in a dark serge suit and a blue necktie, so that the general effect was quiet. Ann greeted him with kindliness and put him with his face to what little light there was. She chose for herself the window-seat. Sylvia had not arrived. She might be a little late—that is, if she came at all.

They talked about the weather for a while. Matthew was of opinion they were going to have some rain. Ann, who was in one of her contra-dictory moods, thought there was frost in the air.

"What did you say to her?" he asked.

"Sylvia? Oh, what you told me," replied Ann. "That you had come to New York to—to look for her."

"What did she say?" he asked.

"Said you'd taken your time about it," retorted Ann.

Matthew looked up with an injured expression.

"It was her own idea that we should never meet," he explained.

"Um!" Ann grunted.

"What do you think yourself she will be like?" she continued. "Have you formed any notion?"

"It is curious," he replied. "I have never been able to conjure up any picture of her until just now."

"Why 'just now'?" demanded Ann.

"I had an idea I should find her here when I opened the door," he answered. "You were standing in the shadow. It seemed to be just what I had expected."

"You would have been satisfied?" she asked.

"Yes," he said.

There was silence for a moment.

"Uncle Ab made a mistake," he continued. "He ought to have sent me away. Let me come home now and then."

"You mean," said Ann, "that if you had seen less of me you might have liked me better?"

"Quite right," he admitted. "We never see the things that are always there."

"A thin, gawky girl with a bad complexion," she suggested. "Would it have been of any use?"

"You must always have been wonderful with those eyes," he answered. "And your hands were beautiful even then."

"I used to cry sometimes when I looked at myself in the glass as a child," she confessed. "My hands were the only thing that consoled me."

"I kissed them once," he told her. "You were asleep, curled up in Uncle Ab's chair."

"I wasn't asleep," said Ann.

She was seated with one foot tucked underneath her. She didn't look a bit grown up.

"You always thought me a fool," he said.

"It used to make me so angry with you," said Ann, "that you seemed to have no go, no ambition in you. I wanted you to wake up—do something. If I had known you were a budding genius—"

"I did hint it to you," said he.

"Oh, of course it was all my fault," said Ann.

He rose. "You think she means to come?" he asked. Ann also had risen.

"Is she so very wonderful?" she asked.

"I may be exaggerating to myself," he answered. "But I am not sure that I could go on with my work without her—not now."

"You forgot her," flashed Ann, "till we happened to quarrel in the cab."

"I often do," he confessed. "Till something goes wrong. Then she comes to me. As she did on that first evening, six years ago. You see, I have been more or less living with her since then," he added with a smile.

"In dreamland," Ann corrected.

"Yes, but in my case," he answered, "the best part of my life is passed in dreamland."

"And when you are not in dreamland?" she demanded. "When you're just irritable, short-tempered, cranky Matthew Pole. What's she going to do about you then?"

"She'll put up with me," said Matthew.

"No she won't," said Ann. "She'll snap your head off. Most of the 'putting up with' you'll have to do."

He tried to get between her and the window, but she kept her face close to the pane.

"You make me tired with Sylvia," she said. "It's about time you did know what she's like. She's just the commonplace, short-tempered, disagreeable-if-she-doesn't-get-her-own-way, unreasonable woman. Only more so."

He drew her away from the window by brute force.

"So you're Sylvia," he said.

"I thought that would get it into your head," said Ann.

It was not at all the way she had meant to break it to him. She had meant the conversation to be chiefly about Sylvia. She had a high opinion of Sylvia, a much higher opinion than she had of Ann Kavanagh. If he proved to be worthy of her—of Sylvia, that is, then, with the whimsical smile that she felt belonged to Sylvia, she would remark quite simply, "Well, what have you got to say to her?"

What had happened to interfere with the programme was Ann Kavanagh. It seemed that Ann Kavanagh had disliked Matthew Pole less than she had thought she did. It was after he had sailed away that little Ann Kavanagh had discovered this. If only he had shown a little more interest in, a little more appreciation of, Ann Kavanagh! He could be kind and thoughtful in a patronising sort of way. Even that would not have mattered if there had been any justification for his airs of superiority.

Ann Kavanagh, who ought to have taken a back seat on this occasion, had persisted in coming to the front. It was so like her.

"Well," she said, "what are you going to say to her?" She did get it in, after all.

"I was going," said Matthew, "to talk to her about Art and Literature, touching, maybe, upon a few other subjects. Also, I might have suggested our seeing each other again once or twice, just to get better acquainted. And then I was going away."

"Why going away?" asked Ann.

"To see if I could forget you."

She turned to him. The fading light was full upon her face.

"I don't believe you could—again," she said.

"No," he agreed. "I'm afraid I couldn't."

"You're sure there's nobody else," said Ann, "that you're in love with. Only us two?"

"Only you two," he said.

She was standing with her hand on old Abner's empty chair. "You've got to choose," she said. She was trembling. Her voice sounded just a little hard.

He came and stood beside her. "I want Ann," he said.

She held out her hand to him.

"I'm so glad you said Ann," she laughed.

THE FAWN GLOVES

Always he remembered her as he saw her first: the little spiritual face, the little brown shoes pointed downwards, their toes just touching the ground; the little fawn gloves folded upon her lap. He was not conscious of having noticed her with any particular attention: a plainly dressed, childish-looking figure alone on a seat between him and the setting sun. Even had he felt curious his shyness would have prevented his deliberately running the risk of meeting her eyes. Yet immediately he had passed her he saw her again, quite clearly: the pale oval face, the brown shoes, and, between them, the little fawn gloves folded one over the other. All down the Broad Walk and across Primrose Hill, he saw her silhouetted against the sinking sun. At least that much of her: the wistful face and the trim brown shoes and the little folded hands; until the sun went down behind the high chimneys of the brewery beyond Swiss Cottage, and then she faded.

She was there again the next evening, precisely in the same place. Usually he walked home by the Hampstead Road. Only occasionally, when the beauty of the evening tempted him, would he take the longer way by Regent Street and through the Park. But so often it made him feel sad, the quiet Park, forcing upon him the sense of his own loneliness.

He would walk down merely as far as the Great Vase, so he arranged with himself. If she were not there—it was not likely that she would be—he would turn back into Albany Street. The newsvendors' shops with their display of the cheaper illustrated papers, the second-hand furniture dealers with their faded engravings and old prints, would give him something to look at, to take away his thoughts from himself. But seeing her in the distance, almost the moment he had entered the gate, it came to him how disappointed he would have been had the seat in front of the red tulip bed been vacant. A little away from her he paused, turning to look at the flowers. He thought that, waiting his opportunity, he might be able to steal a glance at her undetected. Once for a moment he did so, but venturing a second time their eyes met, or he fancied they did, and blushing furiously he hurried past. But again she came with him, or, rather, preceded him. On each empty seat between him and the sinking sun he saw her quite plainly: the pale oval face and the brown shoes, and, between them, the fawn gloves folded one upon the other.

Only this evening, about the small, sensitive mouth there seemed to be hovering just the faintest suggestion of a timid smile. And this time she lingered with him past Queen's Crescent and the Malden Road, till he turned into Carlton Street. It was dark in the passage, and he had to grope his way up the stairs, but with his hand on the door of the bed-sitting room on the third floor he felt less afraid of the solitude that would rise to meet him.

All day long in the dingy back office in Abingdon Street, Westminster, where from ten to six each day he sat copying briefs and petitions, he thought over what he would say to her; tactful beginnings by means of which he would slide into conversation with her. Up Portland Place he would rehearse them to himself. But at Cambridge Gate, when the little fawn gloves came in view, the words would run away, to join him again maybe at the gate into the Chester Road, leaving him meanwhile to pass her with stiff, hurried steps and eyes fixed straight in front of him. And so it might have continued, but that one evening she was no longer at her usual seat. A crowd of noisy children swarmed over it, and suddenly it seemed to him as if the trees and flowers had all turned drab. A terror gnawed at his heart, and he hurried on, more for the need of movement than with any definite object. And just beyond a bed of geraniums that had hidden his view she was seated on a chair, and stopping with a jerk absolutely in front of her, he said, quite angrily:

"Oh! there you are!"

Which was not a bit the speech with which he had intended to introduce himself, but served his purpose just as well—perhaps better.

She did not resent his words or the tone.

"It was the children," she explained. "They wanted to play; so I thought I would come on a little farther."

Upon which, as a matter of course, he took the chair beside her, and it did not occur to either of them that they had not known one another since the beginning, when between St. John's Wood and Albany Street God planted a garden.

Each evening they would linger there, listening to the pleading passion of the blackbird's note, the thrush's call to joy and hope. He loved her gentle ways. From the bold challenges, the sly glances of invitation flashed upon him in the street or from some neighbouring table in the cheap luncheon room he had always shrunk confused and awkward. Her shyness gave him confidence. It was she who was half afraid, whose eyes would fall beneath his gaze, who would tremble at his touch, giving him the delights of manly dominion, of tender authority. It was he who insisted on the aristocratic seclusion afforded by the private chair; who, with the careless indifference of a man to whom pennies were unimportant, would pay for them both. Once on his way through Piccadilly Circus he had paused by the fountain to glance at a great basket of lilies of the valley, struck suddenly by the thought how strangely their little pale petals seemed suggestive of her.

"'Ere y' are, honey. Her favourite flower!" cried the girl, with a grin, holding a bunch towards him.

"How much?" he had asked, vainly trying to keep the blood from rushing to his face.

The girl paused a moment, a coarse, kindly creature.

"Sixpence," she demanded; and he bought them. She had meant to ask him a shilling, and knew he would have paid it. "Same as silly fool!" she called herself as she pocketed the money.

He gave them to her with a fine lordly air, and watched her while she pinned them to her blouse, and a squirrel halting in the middle of the walk watched her also with his head on one side, wondering what was the good of them that she should store them with so much care. She did not thank him in words, but there were tears in her eyes when she turned her face to his, and one of the little fawn gloves stole out and sought his hand. He took it in both his, and would have held it, but she withdrew it almost hurriedly.

They appealed to him, her gloves, in spite of their being old and much mended; and he was glad they were of kid. Had they been of cotton, such as girls of her class usually wore, the thought of pressing his lips to them would have put his teeth on edge. He loved the little brown shoes, that must have been expensive when new, for they still kept their shape. And the fringe of dainty petticoat, always so spotless and with never a tear, and the neat, plain stockings that showed below the closely fitting frock. So often he had noticed girls, showily, extravagantly dressed, but with red bare hands and sloppy shoes. Handsome girls, some of them, attractive enough if you were not of a finicking nature, to whom the little accessories are almost of more importance than the whole.

He loved her voice, so different from the strident tones that every now and then, as some couple, laughing and talking, passed them, would fall upon him almost like a blow; her quick, graceful movements that always brought back to his memory the vision of hill and stream. In her little brown shoes and gloves and the frock which was also of a shade of brown though darker, she was strangely suggestive to him of a fawn. The gentle look, the swift, soft movements that have taken place before they are seen; the haunting suggestion of fear never quite conquered, as if the little nervous limbs were always ready for sudden flight. He called her that one day. Neither of them had ever thought to ask one another's names; it did not seem to matter.

"My little brown fawn," he had whispered, "I am always expecting you to suddenly dig your little heels into the ground and spring away"; and she had laughed and drawn a little closer to him. And even that was just the movement of a fawn. He had known them, creeping near to them upon the hill-sides when he was a child.

There was much in common between them, so they found. Though he could claim a few distant relatives scattered about the North, they were both, for all practical purposes, alone in the world. To her, also, home meant a bed-sitting room—"over there," as she indicated with a wave of the little fawn glove embracing the north-west district generally; and he did not press her for any more precise address.

It was easy enough for him to picture it: the mean, close-smelling street somewhere in the neighbourhood of Lisson Grove, or farther on towards the Harrow Road. Always he preferred to say good-bye to her at some point in the Outer Circle, with its peaceful vista of fine trees and stately houses, watching her little fawn-like figure fading away into the twilight.

No friend or relative had she ever known, except the pale, girlish-looking mother who had died soon after they had come to London. The elderly landlady had let her stay on, helping in the work of the house; and when even this last refuge had failed her, well-meaning folk had interested themselves and secured her employment. It was light and fairly well paid, but there were objections to it, so he gathered, more from her halting silences than from what she said. She had tried for a time to find something else, but it was so difficult without help or resources. There was nothing really to complain about it, except—And then she paused with a sudden clasp of the gloved hands, and, seeing the troubled look in her eyes, he had changed the conversation.

It did not matter; he would take her away from it. It was very sweet to him, the thought of putting a protective arm about this little fragile creature whose weakness gave him strength. He was not always going to be a clerk in an office. He was going to write poetry, books, plays. Already he had earned a little. He told her of his hopes, and her great faith in him gave him new courage. One evening, finding a seat where few people ever passed, he read to her. And she had understood. All unconsciously she laughed in the right places, and when his own voice trembled, and he found it difficult to continue for the lump in his own throat, glancing at her he saw the tears were in her eyes. It was the first time he had tasted sympathy.

And so spring grew to summer. And then one evening a great thing happened. He could not make out at first what it was about her: some little added fragrance that made itself oddly felt, while she herself seemed to be conscious of increased dignity. It was not until he took her hand to say good-bye that he discovered it. There was something different about the feel of her, and, looking down at the little hand that lay in his, he found the reason. She had on a pair of new gloves. They were still of the same fawn colour, but so smooth and soft and cool. They fitted closely without a wrinkle, displaying the slightness and the gracefulness of the hands beneath. The twilight had almost faded, and, save for the broad back of a disappearing policeman, they had the Outer Circle to themselves; and, the sudden impulse coming to him, he dropped on one knee, as they do in plays and story books and some-times elsewhere, and pressed the little fawn gloves to his lips in a long, passionate kiss. The sound of approaching footsteps made him rise hurriedly. She did not move, but her whole body was trembling, and in her eyes was a look that was almost of fear. The approaching footsteps came nearer, but a bend of the road still screened them. Swiftly and in silence she put her arms about his neck and kissed him. It was a strange, cold kiss, but almost fierce, and then without a word she turned and walked away; and he watched her to the corner of Hanover Gate, but she did not look back.

It was almost as if it had raised a barrier between them, that kiss. The next evening she came to meet him with a smile as usual, but in her eyes was still that odd suggestion of lurking fear; and when, seated beside her, he put his hand on hers it seemed to him she shrank away from him. It was an unconscious movement. It brought back to him that haunting memory of hill and stream when some soft-eyed fawn, strayed from her fellows, would let him approach quite close to her, and then, when he put out his hand to caress her, would start away with a swift, quivering movement.

"Do you always wear gloves?" he asked her one evening a little later.

"Yes," she answered, speaking low; "when I'm out of doors."

"But this is not out of doors," he had pleaded. "We have come into the garden. Won't you take them off?"

She had looked at him from under bent brows, as if trying to read him. She did not answer him then. But on the way out, on the last seat close to the gate, she had sat down, motioning him to sit beside her. Quietly she unbuttoned the fawn gloves; drew each one off and laid them aside. And then, for the first time, he saw her hands.

Had he looked at her, seen the faint hope die out, the mute agony in the quiet eyes watching him, he would have tried to hide the disgust, the physical repulsion that showed itself so plainly in his face, in the involuntary movement with which he drew away from her. They were small and shapely with rounded curves, but raw and seared as with hot irons, with a growth of red, angry-coloured warts, and the nails all worn away.

"I ought to have shown them to you before," she said simply as she drew the gloves on again. "It was silly of me. I ought to have known."

He tried to comfort her, but his phrases came meaningless and halting.

It was the work, she explained as they walked on. It made your hands like that after a time. If only she could have got out of it earlier! But now! It was no good worrying about it now.

They parted near to the Hanover Gate, but to-night he did not stand watching her as he had always done till she waved a last good-bye to him just before disappearing; so whether she turned or not he never knew.

He did not go to meet her the next evening. A dozen times his foot-steps led him unconsciously almost to the gate. Then he would hurry away again, pace the mean streets, jostling stupidly against the passers-by. The pale, sweet face, the little nymph-like figure, the little brown shoes kept calling to him. If only there would pass away the horror of those hands! All the artist in him shuddered at the memory of them. Always he had imagined them under the neat, smooth gloves as fitting in with all the rest of her, dreaming of the time when he would hold them in his own, caressing them, kissing them. Would it be possible to forget them, to reconcile oneself to them? He must think—must get away from these crowded streets where faces seemed to grin at him. He remembered that Parliament had just risen, that work was slack in the office. He would ask that he might take his holiday now—the next day. And they had agreed.

He packed a few things into a knapsack. From the voices of the hills and streams he would find counsel.

He took no count of his wanderings. One evening at a lonely inn he met a young doctor. The innkeeper's wife was expecting to be taken with child that night, and the doctor was waiting downstairs till summoned. While they were talking, the idea came to him. Why had he not thought of it? Overcoming his shyness, he put his questions. What work would it be that would cause such injuries? He described them, seeing them before him in the shadows of the dimly lighted room, those poor, pitiful little hands.

Oh! a dozen things might account for it—the doctor's voice sounded callous—the handling of flax, even of linen under certain conditions. Chemicals entered so much nowadays into all sorts of processes and preparations. All this new photography, cheap colour printing, dyeing and cleaning, metal work. Might all be avoided by providing rubber gloves. It ought to be made compulsory. The doctor seemed inclined to hold forth. He interrupted him.

But could it be cured? Was there any hope?

Cured? Hope? Of course it could be cured. It was only local—the effect being confined to the hands proved that. A poisoned condition of the skin aggravated by general poverty of blood. Take her away from it; let her have plenty of fresh air and careful diet, using some such simple ointment or another as any local man, seeing them, would prescribe; and in three or four months they would recover.

He could hardly stay to thank the young doctor. He wanted to get away by himself, to shout, to wave his arms, to leap. Had it been possible he would have returned that very night. He cursed himself for the fancifulness that had prevented his inquiring her address. He could have sent a telegram. Rising at dawn, for he had not attempted to sleep, he walked the ten miles to the nearest railway station, and waited for the train. All day long it seemed to creep with him through the endless country. But London came at last.

It was still the afternoon, but he did not care to go to his room. Leaving his knapsack at the station, he made his way to Westminster. He wanted all things to be unchanged, so that between this evening and their parting it might seem as if there had merely passed an ugly dream; and timing himself, he reached the park just at their usual hour.

He waited till the gates were closed, but she did not come. All day long at the back of his mind had been that fear, but he had driven it away. She was ill, just a headache, or merely tired.

And the next evening he told himself the same. He dared not whisper to himself anything else. And each succeeding evening again. He never remembered how many. For a time he would sit watching the path by which she had always come; and when the hour was long past he would rise and walk towards the gate, look east and west, and then return. One evening he stopped one of the park-keepers and questioned him. Yes, the man remembered her quite well: the young lady with the fawn gloves. She had come once or twice—maybe oftener, the park-keeper could not be sure—and had waited. No, there had been nothing to show that she was in any way upset. She had just sat there for a time, now and then walking a little way and then coming back again, until the closing hour, and then she had gone. He left his address with the park-keeper. The man promised to let him know if he ever saw her there again.

Sometimes, instead of the park, he would haunt the mean streets about Lisson Grove and far beyond the other side of the Edgware Road, pacing them till night fell. But he never found her.

He wondered, beating against the bars of his poverty, if money would have helped him. But the grim, endless city, hiding its million secrets, seemed to mock the thought. A few pounds he had scraped together he spent in advertisements; but he expected no response, and none came. It was not likely she would see them.

And so after a time the park, and even the streets round about it, became hateful to him; and he moved away to another part of London, hoping to forget. But he never quite succeeded. Always it would come back to him when he was not thinking: the broad, quiet walk with its prim trees and gay beds of flowers. And always he would see her seated there, framed by the fading light. At least, that much of her: the little spiritual face, and the brown shoes pointing downwards, and between them the little fawn gloves folded upon her lap.

www.ingramcontent.com/pod-product-compliance
Lightning Source LLC
Chambersburg PA
CBHW020250150626
46552CB00020B/755